KT-548-692

OTFORD LIBRARY

13. SEP 06.

05. JAN 07

2 8 MAR 2009

WITHDRAWN

2 8 JAN 2012

2 9 JUL 2023

2 5 JAN 2023

SEV

Books should be returned or renewed by the
last date stamped above.

Kent
County
Council

00884\DTP\RN\04.05   LIB 7

CUSTOMER SERVICE EXCELLENCE

C152905043

GIGOLO

GIGOLO

Raymond Haigh

CHIVERS
THORNDIKE

This Large Print book is published by BBC Audiobooks Ltd, Bath, England and by Thorndike Press®, Waterville, Maine, USA.

Published in 2006 in the U.K. by arrangement with Robert Hale Limited.

Published in 2006 in the U.S. by arrangement with Robert Hale Limited.

U.K. Hardcover ISBN 1–4056–3573–8 (Chivers Large Print)
U.K. Softcover ISBN 1–4056–3574–6 (Camden Large Print)
U.S. Softcover ISBN 0–7862–8206–1 (British Favorites)

Copyright © Raymond Haigh 2005

The right of Raymond Haigh to be identified as author of this work has been asserted by him in accordance with the Copyright, Designs and Patents Act 1988.

All rights reserved.

The text of this Large Print edition is unabridged.
Other aspects of the book may vary from the original edition.

Set in 16 pt. New Times Roman.

Printed in Great Britain on acid-free paper.

British Library Cataloguing in Publication Data available

Library of Congress Cataloging-in-Publication Data

Haigh, Raymond, 1937–
    Gigolo / by Raymond Haigh.—Large print ed.
        p.   cm.
    "Thorndike Press large print British favorites."—T.p. verso.
    ISBN 0–7862–8206–1 (lg. print : sc : alk. paper)
    1. Women private investigators—England—Fiction. 2. Large
    type books. I. Title.
PR6058.A418G54 2005
823'.92—dc22   2005024764

KENT
ARTS & LIBRARIES

C152905043

GIGOLO

CHAPTER ONE

Samantha clicked open the attaché case and lifted out the automatic pistol. The topmost photograph was exposed now, and she studied, for a few moments, the image of a mature woman snuggling close to an extravagantly handsome young man. She would have to use the gun. Short of the kind of intimacy she'd neither the time nor the inclination for, there was no other way he could be persuaded to tell her the things she needed to know.

The gun's weight was comforting. Samantha checked the magazine and the movement of the breech, then caressed its gleaming blackness with the yellow duster that had been wrapped around it. Reaching into a pocket in the lid of the case, she pulled out the silencer and screwed it on to the muzzle. The weapon was unbalanced now, but that wouldn't be a problem in the hotel room, and its greater length made it more intimidating.

Soft carpets and silk drapes in muted shades of blue, exotic veneers and inlays, made the room and its furnishings sumptuous. Glancing around, she considered tactics. If she sat on the small sofa while he got drinks from the mini-bar she could look him over without it appearing too obvious. And when the interrogation began, she had to be close to the

1

door with him on the far side of the bed.

Samantha laid the gun back on top of the photographs, checked the camera, then lowered the lid of the case and carried it over to a small writing desk located between the bed and the door.

Her watch showed six-fifty. He was due in ten minutes. He could be waiting in the foyer now, and she still had the bathroom door to fix.

Taking a small screwdriver from a leather pouch of tools and lock-picks in the attaché case, she crossed over to the bathroom and attacked the grub screw that secured the door handle to its shaft. The fittings were new and the screw turned easily. Samantha withdrew it and dropped it in a soap dish recessed into marbled blue tiles. When she tugged at the outer handle, the shaft began to slide out of the lock. She pressed it back in place.

The summer evening light was still strong. She drew the drapes across the windows, then switched on bedside, desk and wall lamps. Isolated now, shut off from the world, secret: the diffused glow from the lamps made the room seem intimate and inviting.

Samantha dropped the voice recorder into her evening purse, stepped into some suede and snakeskin Alexander McQueen shoes, then viewed her reflection in a mirror next to the door. Her grey Dior suit was stylish but not eye-catching. Its exquisitely tailored little

2

jacket fitted snugly around her waist, and some cleavage showed between the lapels.

Smoothing the pencil skirt over her hips, she stepped out into the corridor, hooked the "Do Not Disturb" sign over the door handle, and headed for the lift.

*   *   *

He was waiting in a smart little cocktail lounge off the foyer. He looked towards her and smiled as she approached, then rose to his feet and held out a hand.

'I think you're the lady I'm supposed to meet.'

'Mr Noble . . . Mr James Noble?' Samantha placed her hand in his. It was warm and dry and he held her fingers gently while they looked one another over.

He was tall, but not too tall, perhaps a fraction-of-an-inch short of six feet. Dark curly hair, perfectly barbered; clean shaven, broad shouldered, with a slim but athletic build. He wouldn't be easy to intimidate.

'I gather we're having dinner together.' His baritone voice was genial, his smile pleasant. 'May I get you a drink before we start out?'

'I have to finish getting ready. The table's booked for eight and the restaurant's quite close so we've plenty of time. Perhaps we could go up to my room and have a drink there . . .'

3

Samantha watched his face. His expression remained serious and attentive. He didn't smirk at her suggestion that they go up to her room. And the photograph didn't do him justice. In the flesh he seemed very self-assured, almost formidable. She was beginning to feel edgy. She had to move things along quickly.

'Whatever you wish,' he said genially. 'But I can't imagine what more you have to do to get ready. You look very elegant.'

Samantha smiled. He was working hard, doing his best to give satisfaction, maybe hoping for a repeat booking.

He moved a chair aside for her, followed her out of the bar and across the foyer, and punched the button for the lift.

'I don't know your name.'

'You can call me Jane.' She was looking up at the illuminated floor numbers, willing the lift to descend faster.

'Forgive me, but you don't look like a Jane.'

Samantha turned, eyebrows raised. He was smiling down at her. She heard the lift doors rumble open and they stepped inside.

'Which floor?'

'Third,' she said, and watched him press the button as she asked, 'What's wrong with Jane?'

'It's so ordinary and your appearance is so unusual, so out-of-the-ordinary.'

'You mean I look freaky?'

'Oh God, no,' he protested. 'I'm sorry. I put

4

that very badly. I wanted to say you're beautiful in such a special way.'

Samantha raised an eyebrow and went on looking at him steadily, trying to intensify his confusion, undermine that calm confidence she found rather worrying.

He seemed genuinely embarrassed by his faux pas. 'Your hair,' he floundered on, 'it's so thick and lustrous and black, and if your eyes were dark instead of that incredibly vivid green you'd make a perfect Cleopatra with it cut that way.'

'You don't have to try quite so hard, James.'

'Am I forgiven?' He was leaning against the wall of the lift, arms folded, smiling across at her.

She didn't answer. Just went on looking him up and down, slowly, in a detached almost clinical way. His double-breasted blue pinstripe suit was handmade, like his gleaming black shoes. The shirt was freshly laundered; the blue silk tie and the handkerchief peeping out of his breast pocket seemed brand new. Gold cuff links and a gold Rolex added the finishing touches. Samantha wondered if they were presents from satisfied clients.

'Do you work in the City?' he asked.

Samantha nodded. 'Options and futures at Heckler and Koch on Canary Wharf.'

She watched his face. His expression didn't change. He was still gazing at her in that genial, attentive way. He hadn't picked up on

5

her use of the German gunmaker's name for her fictitious finance house.

The lift lurched to a stop. He smiled and stood back whilst she stepped out on to deep pile carpet and moved on down the corridor.

'May I ask you a personal question?'

She glanced up at him. 'You can ask but I might not answer.'

'Do you have laryngitis?'

Samantha laughed. 'Of course I don't have laryngitis.'

'Then you've the sexiest voice I've ever heard in my entire life.'

'First you say I look freaky, now you're saying I've got a peculiar voice.'

'You know what I mean,' he insisted. 'It's . . . it's like leaves rustling in the breeze on a hot summer night. I could listen to it forever.'

Corny, Samantha thought, but ten-out-of-ten for effort. She was still laughing softly when they arrived at the door of her room.

She reached into her purse, switched on the voice recorder, then took out a magnetic card and slid it into the lock. She pressed the handle and pushed open the door, set the 'Do Not Disturb' sign swinging, semaphoring its blatant message.

'Come on in.' She went over to the writing desk, placed her purse next to the attaché case and kicked off her shoes before heading for the sofa. 'Let's have a drink while I finish getting ready. The mini-bar's over here.'

'What can I get you?' He tugged open the refrigerator door.

'Whisky and a little water.'

'Your job, options and futures, high finance; it sounds very demanding . . . Would you like ice in it?'

'Ice is fine. It's boring and political rather than demanding.'

He brought over the drinks: a generous whisky for her, the remainder of the mineral water for him. 'May I?' He gestured at the seat next to hers on the sofa.

Samantha patted the cushion with her hand, her crimson nails like flecks of blood on the blue fabric. 'Of course,' she said, eyeing the water in his glass, disappointed because she'd been hoping a couple of strong drinks would make him less alert.

'You don't want to talk about your work, do you?' he said softly.

Samantha took the tiniest sip at her whisky. 'I'd much rather talk about you?'

'There's hardly anything to know.'

'You seem very cultured. Tell me a little about your education.'

He shrugged and his smile faded. 'Went to a small prep school until I was thirteen, then to a public school. That's when my education really began.' His voice had become bitter. It was obvious he didn't feel well disposed to the public school system. 'Went to Oxford after that.'

7

'Why public school?' She was dripping acid into the cut.

'My mother died. My father thought it would be the best thing.'

'I imagine you got a good degree.'

He laughed. 'This is all wrong. We should be talking about you. You're the only person that matters tonight.' He sipped at the water. 'English. I managed a first.'

'That explains how you can flatter women in such a cultivated way.'

'I don't flatter. I compliment them. There's always some feature one can be complimentary about.' He wasn't smiling now. She seemed to have offended him.

Samantha gazed at him without speaking. The sofa was small but he was managing to keep his broad shoulders and long limbs well clear of her. He seemed to be unsure of her; trying to work out what she expected of him.

'What made you become an escort?'

The blunt question increased his discomfort. He looked down at his glass, shrugged, and said, 'I enjoy the company of women. I don't much care to be with men. And women don't seem to find me unpleasant. It was a natural career choice.'

'I suppose quite a number of them repeat the pleasure?'

He glanced up, his eyes suddenly wary. 'You're the woman I'm with tonight, Jane, and I want to make your evening as memorable as

I can. I don't want to even think about another woman, and I'd certainly never talk about one behind her back.'

The total discretion of the perfect gentleman and high-class whore: there was no way he'd just tell her what she wanted to know. He had to be intimidated. And she'd disconcerted him; made him wary of her. On reflection, that wasn't good. She needed him relaxed and unsuspecting.

Samantha gave him an apologetic smile. 'I'm sorry. You've been nothing but kind and I'm being unpleasant. I'll get ready, then we can . . .'

He laid his hand on her arm. 'Please, don't apologize. There's nothing to apologize for. You're probably tired after a rotten day, and anyway, your curiosity's perfectly natural. Finish your drink and we'll go out and dine. You look utterly perfect just the way you are.'

Tired after a rotten day; perfect just the way you are. He certainly knew the right buttons to press.

Samantha sank back into the cushions. She'd have to make her move soon. She took another sip at her drink, then asked, 'What did you specialize in, at Oxford I mean?'

'Romanticism particularly interested me.' Grey eyes were looking at her intently. He seemed to be trying to understand her, to adjust his manner, his behaviour, to her mood.

Samantha smiled. 'Man in a state of nature,

the noble savage, disdain for getting and spending: seems appropriate.'

'You've a knowledge of Romanticism? I'm impressed.' He seemed pleased.

'Not really,' she said. 'Just the odd snippet I've picked up here and there. While we're having dinner you can give me a few verses of Byron. How about "Childe Harold's Pilgrimage"?'

He laughed softly. 'Now I know you're teasing me. You really do know something about Romanticism.'

Samantha met his gaze. He'd suddenly relaxed and was at ease with her. That was good. She'd take him unawares.

'May I kiss you . . . ?'

Samantha's eyebrows lifted. She ought not to be shocked: bringing him to her room, the 'Do Not Disturb' sign on the door, sharing the small sofa with him.

'. . . I'd like to very much,' he murmured softly.

She didn't say anything, just gazed at him, eyes wide, lips parted.

He leant forward. She felt his arm encircling her shoulders, his hand curving around her waist. The kiss was tender and expert and rather prolonged. Up close his body was warm and fragrant. A night of this was costing her clients more than two-weeks' wages for most working women. And it wasn't unpleasant. She was disconcerted and losing focus now. She had to act.

Samantha touched his cheek and gazed into his eyes. 'Why don't you get undressed?' she whispered huskily.

Nothing in his expression betrayed any surprise. She could have been asking him to get her another drink. He rose to his feet, removed his jacket draped it carefully over the arm of the sofa, then sauntered towards the bed while he removed his tie and unfastened the cuffs of his shirt. He sat at the foot of the king-sized bed and, while he unlaced his shoes, began to talk to her about some opera he'd enjoyed the previous night at Covent Garden.

Samantha watched him put socks inside shoes before sliding them under the bed, then he rose and peeled off his shirt. The lean, tanned body was spectacular. Hours at the gym and under a sun lamp, probably some painful hair waxing; it was clearly an asset he cosseted. In the subdued lighting his musculature was as clearly defined as a drawing in an anatomy textbook. She couldn't despise the women who paid to caress and be caressed by that body; who'd allowed themselves to be seduced for a while by all the counterfeit sincerity and cultivated charm.

He walked around the bed. Right-handed, he'd instinctively headed for the side farthest from the door and the writing desk. So far, things were working out well. He drew back the coverlet and smiled across at her in a

11

wordless invitation to join him.

Unbuttoning her jacket, she moved towards the bed. When she was facing him across the expanse of white linen she slowly opened it, drew it over her shoulders and let it fall to the floor. She watched his gaze drop to breasts nestling in a butterfly tracery of black silk and lace; it remained there while he pushed down blue-striped boxer shorts and kicked them from his legs. He was magnificently priapic. For a moment she felt flattered, then reminded herself that this was his stock in trade, the thing he did for a living.

Samantha turned her back to him, used her body to conceal the attaché case whilst she lifted the lid, took out the gun and got it in both hands, hiding it from him like a dentist conceals the hypodermic from a patient. Then, arms outstretched, she swung the gun in an arc, spreading her feet a little as she turned and pointed it at his chest.

He let out an embarrassed little laugh, raised his hands in protest as he said, 'I don't do kinky or bondage, Jane, just normal sex.'

'This isn't kinky sex, James,' Samantha snapped. 'It's your brains all over the wall if you don't be a good boy and do as you're told.'

'Hey, what is this? You can't . . .'

'Get your hands behind your head and face the wall.'

'What's happening here? Why are you doing this to me?'

Reproach and anger were mingling with the surprise in his voice now.

'Do it!' Samantha demanded.

'Why should I? What the hell's the matter with you?'

He didn't seem scared. It wasn't going to be easy to intimidate him. She swung the gun down and pointed it at his groin, then made her voice menacingly urgent as she said, 'If you don't do as I say you'll lose your business equipment and get an arsehole big enough for an elephant to shit through. So do it.'

His eyes, glaring at her across the bed, the set of his mouth, were telling her how much she'd disappointed him, how much he loathed her.

She jerked the gun and screamed, *'Do it!'*

He did as she said.

Without taking her eyes off his muscular back, the firm tightly clenched buttocks, she reached into the case, picked out a digital camera, and took a couple of pictures.

'Why the hell are you behaving like this? I do what I do because I really like women, then you come along and start acting as if you've more testosterone than Tarzan.'

'So, you really liked women until I came along. Stop whining and turn to face the bedside table. Keep your hands behind your head and don't try anything or I might get nervous and blow half your arse off.'

'I adore women, I don't just like them. Five

years in that sodding public school: a lunatic asylum full of bloody sadists. Bullied all day and tormented all night. I loathe men. I loathe the bastards almost as much as I loathe ball-breaking bitches like you.'

'Don't look at me, look at the wall,' Samantha snarled, then took two more pictures.

'Now face me. And get away from the bed. Get back against the wall.' His impressive manhood had subsided to an engorged tumescence. Gun in one hand, camera in the other, she took frontal pictures then slid the camera back into the attaché case and resumed her two-handed, arms-outstretched hold on the gun.

'Get down on your knees.'

'Christ, what are you going to do to me?' His voice was shaking.

'Do it!'

He knelt in front of the bed.

Samantha took the topmost photograph from the case and tossed it over. 'That's photograph number one,' Samantha snapped for the voice recorder. 'Do you recognize the woman? Has she been a client?'

'I refuse to discuss the women I've . . .'

'I don't think I'm getting through to you, James.' She made her voice menacing. 'This is a large bore pistol. At this range you'd get blown apart. And it's got a silencer. When I pull the trigger it just goes phut; quieter than a

14

bishop breaking wind. I've come from nowhere to the big city. No one can trace me when I leave. You're seriously vulnerable.'

He was glaring at her across the bed.

'What are you?' she demanded.

'Vulnerable,' he repeated sulkily.

'OK.' She tugged at the breech of the pistol, watched him twitch when she let it spring back with a metallic clatter. 'Tell me what I want to know.'

He glared at her for a moment longer, then swallowed hard and looked down at the photograph. 'I had lunch with her a couple of times, then we spent the afternoon in the Ibis Hotel. Another time we spent the night together.'

'When?'

'I can't remember when.'

'Try.'

'It was just after New Year; the first and second weeks in January and maybe the first week in February.'

'And what happened in the bedrooms?'

'What always happens in hotel bedrooms? We made love.'

'What's love got to do with it?' Samantha spat. 'You had sex; you copulated. How many times?'

'At least twice in the afternoons. When she stayed over we made love through the night. I can't remember how many times. I just go on until the lady asks me to stop.'

Samantha drew another photograph from the case. 'This is photograph number two,' she announced for the recorder, then flicked it towards him. 'Tell me about her.'

He reached across the sheets and picked it up. 'Barbara; she's really sweet, always laughing. I meet her about once a month, usually on a Monday evening. She books in at the Carlton and we have dinner together.'

'And?'

'And what?' he demanded petulantly.

'And what do you do after having dinner with a woman old enough to be your mother?'

His chin was quivering now. 'You bitch,' he muttered. 'You bloody ball-breaking little bitch.'

Samantha jerked the gun. 'Tell me.'

'We make love through the night. Like I said, until she asks me to stop. I don't count the number of times I give her pleasure; I wouldn't be so vulgar.' His face suddenly hardened with anger, 'And you might copulate,' he growled, 'but I make love.'

She tossed another photograph at him and the ritual began again. When the last image was lying amongst the pile on the bed she snapped, 'Get up and go inside the bathroom. *Move!*' She gestured with the gun but remained where she was while he stumbled, naked and stiff from kneeling, across the room.

'What the hell are you going to do with me

now?'

'Stop whining. And keep your hands behind your head.'

Just before he moved out of sight, Samantha darted across the room, keeping the gun leveled at him. 'Shut the door,' she demanded. 'Push it hard.'

The latch clicked. She stepped over and tugged at the handle. It pulled away, drawing out the spindle, and she heard the other handle clatter on to the bathroom floor.

'What is this?' said a muffled voice, followed by banging on the door.

Samantha put her mouth close to the panelling. 'Sit there for half-an-hour. If I hear a sound I'll start shooting blind through the door.'

She lifted his jacket from the sofa and found his wallet. A driver's licence gave his real name as Gavin Rudd and recorded a North London address. She kept one of his agency cards.

In another inside pocket she found a small diary crammed with initials, times and places. He'd used a simple short-hand to record details of the women's likes and dislikes in matters of food, drink, conversation and sex. She replaced the wallet; kept the diary.

Gathering up the photographs from the bed, she checked she had all fifteen, then returned them to the attaché case. His trousers were neatly folded over the back of a chair. She reached inside the pockets, felt car and house keys and some loose change. She tossed it all on to the bed.

There were no sounds from the bathroom. He must have sensed his ordeal was almost over, been listening to her movements, waiting for the outer door to slam.

Samantha picked up her jacket, slipped it on and fastened the buttons while she stepped into her shoes. Before switching off the voice recorder, she murmured, 'Investigation completed, leaving premises at,' she glanced at her watch, 'eight p.m. on Friday the fourth of July.' Stepping out into the corridor, she tossed the 'Do Not Disturb' sign into the room.

Down in the foyer she made for the reception desk.

'Madam?' The morning suit was immaculate, the voice refined and deferential. It was that kind of hotel.

'I've been called away unexpectedly, but the gentleman's staying on. Could you have a meal taken up for him in about half an hour?'

'Certainly, madam. What would the gentleman like?'

'Mmm . . . A large steak, medium-rare, some French fries and assorted vegetables.'

'Very good madam.'

'Oh, and three bottles of Becks, nicely chilled. There's no beer in the bar.'

'I'm most sorry about that, Madam, but I'll have some sent up.'

'The room and breakfast were paid for when I booked. Perhaps I could settle for the meal now, while someone brings my car around to the front?'

'But of course.' He turned and snapped his fingers, whispered an instruction to a younger flunky in the regulation black jacket and pinstripes.

'And would you tell the waiter to go straight into the room. My partner said he was going to take a shower and he might not hear him knocking.'

Fifteen minutes later, Samantha was cruising down sunlit London streets, deftly manoeuvring the silver Ferrari Modena through the traffic as she headed for Potters Bar and the North.

CHAPTER TWO

Hugh Dixon turned, loped across the deserted dual carriageway, then headed up a road that rose through an area of old terrace housing on the eastern side of Barfield. He was moving effortlessly, his breathing regular and controlled, and he felt no tiredness despite the lateness of the hour. Street lamps were lower powered and more widely spaced here. He was running through stretches of darkness punctuated by pools of light, the rubber soles of his trainers squishing over flagstones wet with gentle summer rain.

His runs had become a nightly ritual. Sleep was impossible without this release of physical energy. The rhythm of the exercise calmed him, blurring the edges of his frustration, helping him cope with all the tormenting thoughts and images that crowded his mind.

Hugh padded on, T-shirt and shorts soaked with rain, past the school, down a long stretch of unlit road between open fields; and then he was running through an estate of small inter-wars semis. He was almost at her house, Emma Turner's house, now.

He'd started the nightly run in April, about a week after he'd met her at that sales promotion evening. When the promotion was over they'd had a couple of drinks together and he'd driven her home. What had happened then had changed him. The juvenile little tarts he used to pick up in clubs and pubs hadn't interested him after that.

He turned into a tree-lined crescent where bigger detached houses were separated from the road by deep gardens. He could see the huge gable over the bay windows of her house now and, as he drew closer, the shiny red door with its oval panel of stained glass and the unlit carriage lamps on either side of the porch.

Pausing beneath a roadside tree, he gazed up at the curtains drawn across her bedroom window. Emma would be in there; fragrant, fabulous Emma. Her nakedness had been a revelation: small waist curving out to wide hips, soft plump thighs, the large breasts that had been such a wonderful surprise. And she'd been so responsive, participating rather than submitting, encouraging him with words and caresses and the movement of her body.

Her husband would be lying with her now. Hugh had never met him. He was thankful for that. Perhaps they were . . . He clenched his fists, screwed his eyes tight shut in an effort to block the unbearable images from his mind. It was at moments like this he was able to admit to himself that he was obsessed, a sad bastard besotted by a woman who no longer wanted to know him. The frustration was unbearable. He had to give it another try; phone her again tomorrow or, better still, call and see her at her office.

He was beginning to ache. If he stood there any longer he'd never resume the effortless rhythm of his run. Pushing himself away from the tree, he began to move steadily around the crescent, heading back to his flat on the other side of town.

*   *   *

Emma Turner tugged at her desk drawer, took out the packet of aspirin and pressed a couple of tablets from the pack. It was all getting too

21

much: this trouble with Darren Blake, Adam walking out on her. And being chief quantity surveyor was turning out to be something of a poisoned chalice. It was still very much a man's world and every one of her staff was a man, constantly challenging her, delighting in every slip she made. And that Muslim the committee had forced her to take on; he did as he was told but she could almost feel his resentment at taking instructions from a woman, showing his contempt for her with that dumb insolence he'd elevated to an art form.

Emma dropped the tablets into a cardboard cup, added a little mineral water, then stirred the mixture with a pencil until the fizzing stopped. She swallowed it at a gulp, grimacing at the bitterness.

And she was missing Adam. His leaving had been a shock. She hadn't thought he had it in him. She still couldn't make much sense of the rambling conversation they'd had when he'd told her he was leaving. All that business about brother and sister relationships, about needing a physical display of affection; being better off out of the house because her nearness, sharing the same bed, just made him more aware of his needs, more aware of how sterile their relationship had become.

She wondered if he'd heard something about her little conference flings, or if one of the neighbours had seen that sales rep, Hugh Dixon, leaving the house and said something.

She dismissed the idea. Adam hardly ever saw the neighbours, let alone spoke to them, and he was so bloody trusting it wasn't true. God, he was naïve: utterly pathetic.

She'd nursed him through his redundancy, kept him for a year while he got his antique business going. According to her daughter, Ruth, it was doing quite well. She wasn't surprised: he could fix anything so the restoration work wouldn't be a problem for him. That was one thing she did miss; all the jobs he did around the house. Dammit, she missed him just being there when she got home.

Perhaps she should have tried to be more accommodating, just lain back and thought about office problems while he fiddled around and grunted and gasped his way through what, for him, passed for lovemaking. She shuddered. Who did she think she was kidding? He'd become more than boringly unattractive; she'd begun to find him physically repellent.

The phone rang. She lifted the handset.

'Mrs Turner? It's Monica here. Mr Jackson asked if you could come up to his office.'

'When does the old goat want me to come up?'

Monica giggled. They shared a womanly contempt for the borough architect. 'He said right away.'

'Any idea what its about? Do I need any

papers or anything?'

'He didn't say.' The secretary was still giggling.

Emma knocked before entering the only decent office in the building. Framed photographs of projects lined the walls and a model of the new Ethnic Minorities Welfare Centre covered the top of a mahogany plan chest. A large drawing board was arranged in front of one of the long windows. Its cover was drawn down and strewn with papers. Stanley Jackson didn't do much drawing any more.

'Emma! Come in and sit down.'

She sat, decorously, on the visitor's chair, knees covered by the pleated skirt of her black business suit, and eyed the bespectacled man over piles of papers heaped on the massive partnership desk. Moustache and tiny goatee beard neatly trimmed, he was wearing a blue-striped shirt and red bow tie. Emma guessed he was in sombre mood. On more up-beat days he usually wore a pink or lilac shirt and a polka-dot tie.

She raised an eyebrow.

Stanley Jackson coughed. 'How are the documents going for the Chase Lane Comprehensive extension?'

'OK. The team taking off the quantities need the joinery details, but if Fergus gets the drawings over this week we should be out to tender before the end of the month.'

'On schedule?'

'A week early, actually. I thought I'd add it to the tendering period; give the contractors a little more time.'

Jackson nodded. 'Good. That's good.' He linked long, thin fingers and leant on the paper-strewn desk. 'Grimson, one of the directors of Bartlets, phoned me last night. In a lather about this month's interim payment. Said it was less than twenty thousand. Going on about some correction for excavation in rock.'

Emma realized then why he'd called her to his office and began to feel uneasy. 'The rock's been over-measured and Bartlets had an enormous rate in for it. I tried to get them to adjust it before we signed the contract, but they wouldn't budge.'

'Over-measured?' Jackson's plummy voice was tetchy. 'Your surveyor measured it with their surveyor, I don't see how there can be a discrepancy.'

'Exactly,' Emma said. 'That's why I've suspended Darren.'

'Darren?'

'The quantity surveyor who's dealing with the job. Internal Audit are currently doing a check with Markham.'

'Markham?'

'Judas Priest,' Emma muttered to herself. 'The stupid old goat hardly knows what day it is.' Out loud she said, 'Markham, the new senior quantity surveyor we set on a couple of months ago. You sat in on the interviews.'

'Oh, that Markham.' He frowned at her over rimless spectacles. 'How much have you clawed back then?'

'A hundred-and-fifty thousand.'

'Bloody hell! There's not that much rock in Barfield Borough.'

'Most of it was supposed to be in the off-site sewer trenches, but I checked the ground survey with the engineers and rock doesn't start until two metres down. That set the alarm bells ringing. When I had a look on site I knew there was no way there could have been all that excavation in rock.'

'What did what's-his-name, the job QS, say?'

'Darren said the rock outcrops at the bottom of the site and they'd had to cut into it for the boiler room and most of the foul drainage.'

'And would that account for so much rock?'

Emma shook her head. 'There's only one possible explanation: Darren's been getting back-handers.'

'We've never had anything like this before.' Jackson was white around the mouth and his hands were shaking.

'Not that we know of,' Emma said wryly. 'And I'm afraid there's more.'

'More? What do you mean, more?'

'The engineers called for some heavy reinforcement in the strip footings. It's been

26

paid for but I don't think it's there.'

The borough architect eyed her bleakly. 'Not there?'

Did he have to repeat everything she said? They ought to call him Pretty Polly, not the Old Goat. 'When I went on site there were no bars projecting from the last concrete pour. I think we should run a metal detector over the foundations. And there are some huge pre-cast concrete blocks being craned in to retain the bank at the top of the site. They look OK, but I think we should do a check on them while we're at it.'

'What the hell's the clerk of works been doing?'

Emma shrugged. 'Perhaps he's in on the scam.'

Jackson flopped back in his chair. 'I could have done without this, Emma. Things are so dammed sensitive now: all these ethnic minority people on the council, clamouring for their schemes to be top priority, always moaning about discrimination. And the bloody Conservatives just want the department closed down so they can farm the work out amongst friends and supporters. Remember what happened to you and your section last Christmas?'

Emma looked down at her hands.

'Written notices of redundancy,' he reminded her. 'If the government funding for the ethnic minorities projects hadn't come

27

through half the department would have had to go by Easter.' He turned and gazed out of the window for a moment, then muttered bitterly, 'Ethnic minorities: we're the bloody ethnic minority now.' He glanced back at her. 'Thanks Emma. That'll be all. Keep me posted. I don't like audit having been brought in; we should have dealt with this ourselves. If we're not careful I could lose control of it.'

Emma pushed herself out of the chair. 'Will you have a word with Bruce?'

'Bruce?'

'Bruce Benson, the project architect. About checking the foundation reinforcement.'

He nodded absently. 'Ask Monica to call him up to my office right away.'

Emma was just about to step through the doorway when he called, 'Thanks Emma. For spotting it, I mean. It's bad enough as it is, but if you'd not found out . . .'

Emma peered through the next door along. 'He wants Bruce Benson in right away.'

Monica, white-haired and homely, looked up. 'I'll give him a ring. How's his majesty?'

Emma grimaced. 'Not pleased.'

'There was a call for you while you were in there; from your daughter's school.' Monica flicked through a notepad. 'Sister Annunciata. Said she'd like you to give her a call before twelve. She said it wasn't anything to worry about or I'd have come in with the message.'

Back in her office, headache slightly worse,

28

Emma leafed through her organizer, found the telephone number of her daughter's school, and dialed. Someone went to find the headmistress and presently an Irish voice came on the line.

'Mrs Turner?'

'Sister Annunciata?'

'That's right, dear. Thanks for calling back. I'd like to have a little chat with you and your husband about Ruth.'

'Is there a problem?'

A little laugh came down the line. 'No, no, nothing like that, Mrs Turner, quite the reverse in fact. But we need to talk and I think it would be best if Ruth didn't know.'

'Could we discuss it over the phone?'

'No, not really. It's rather delicate. We need to meet.'

Emma's curiosity was aroused. 'When do you suggest?'

'Why not today?'

'It could be difficult, unless you can see me in my lunch hour.'

'And what time would that be?'

'It's pretty flexible, but anything from twelve onwards.'

'How about twelve thirty?'

'That would be fine,' Emma said, then, suddenly remembering, added, 'I'm afraid I couldn't bring my husband along, he's working away and . . .'

'Don't worry, Mrs Turner. I think it might

be better with just the two of us. And you'll be missing your lunch so we'll have tea and sandwiches together. Come to the convent, not the school. That way Ruth won't bump into you.'

Emma replaced the phone. Red carpet treatment: what had she done to deserve that?

There was a tap on the half-open door. One of the new trainees was eyeing her nervously.

'There's been a couple of calls for you, Mrs Turner. A brick rep,' he glanced down at a slip of paper.

'Hugh Dixon?' Emma prompted.

'Yeah, that's right. He asked if you'd phone him on his mobile. I got the number.' The trainee approached the desk and laid the paper on the blotter.

'He needs the project architects. I don't select the bricks. Didn't someone tell him that?'

'Mr Markham did, but the rep said it was about a price they'd quoted. Said it was urgent.'

'Thanks Jeremy.'

He headed towards the door.

'Oh, Jeremy.'

He glanced back.

'Don't wear jeans and an open necked shirt in the office. It's not professional. Shirt and tie and a suit.'

'Sorry, Mrs Turner.'

*   *   *

'Do you take sugar, Mrs Turner?'

'No, thanks.' Emma watched the matronly, grey-haired woman pour tea from a brown pot covered with a blue knitted cosy.

The nuns at St Mary's still looked like nuns: black calf-length dresses with starched white collars and cuffs, and black wimples edged with white around the face. And, even in summer, heavily darned black cardigans.

'Help yourself to sandwiches; there's chicken and ham.'

'What's Ruth been getting up to, Sister? What's the problem?'

'There isn't a problem. Is the sun in your eyes? This parlour does catch the sun. I'll draw the . . .'

'I'm fine, Sister.' Emma sank back into the chintz and smiled at the old nun across a square of patterned carpet. Bookcases lined the walls and a huge oak fireplace with barley-sugar columns almost reached the ceiling.

'Tell me,' Sister Annunciata began, 'have you noticed any change in Ruth recently, anything different about her?'

Emma shrugged and began to feel guilty. She'd been so preoccupied with her work. Adam walking out didn't seem to have affected Ruth as much as it might. He'd been away buying stock in the months before he left, and he'd only moved across town so Ruth could see him whenever she wanted. 'Nothing

I wouldn't put down to her age,' Emma said evasively. 'She's sometimes a little remote, perhaps.'

Sister Annunciata sipped at the hot tea. 'Remote: well now. And what would you say if I told you she wants to enter the order?'

Emma lowered cup to saucer and slid them on to the table. 'Enter the . . .'

'That's right, Mrs Turner. Enter the order; become a nun.'

'I really don't know. This is so unexpected.'

'We noticed a kind of transformation in her about Easter. She seemed to mature, spend less time giggling with the other girls. She even drifted away from her best friend, the Langton girl.' The old nun was eyeing her shrewdly but not unkindly. She sipped at her tea again, then said, 'I gather this has come as a surprise?'

Emma laughed. 'Frankly, yes. I'm very surprised.' She and Adam had only gone to church for a year so they could get Ruth into the school. Once she'd been accepted, they'd abandoned the pretence. 'Has she talked to you about it, Sister?'

'Once or twice. It's Sister Winifred she confides in. She takes the sixth-form girls for religion and philosophy. She's very inspirational.'

'You think Sister Winifred's encouraged her?'

Sister Annunciata shook her head. 'No, not at all. She wouldn't do that. God plants the seed. If Ruth really has a vocation He'll

32

nurture it. As I said, we noticed she'd become more devotional around Easter. She joins us in the chapel for the Angelus and the Rosary, and she goes to mass here whenever she can.'

Emma's feelings of guilt deepened. She always had a lie-in on Sunday. Ruth was up long before her. She must have been going to the early mass at St Bede's. She hadn't even been aware of that. 'Has Ruth explained her reasons to Sister Winifred?'

'When she teased her about becoming more devout and asked her why, Ruth said the idea had been growing for a long time, but something she'd seen had finally convinced her. Sister Winifred asked her if she thought she'd had a vision of some sort: teenage girls who go through a devotional phase can have all sorts of silly fancies, but she said it was nothing like that.'

'Something she'd seen?'

'We didn't probe, Mrs Turner. The call to the religious life is a mysterious thing. It could have been a picture in a book, something on television; who knows?'

Emma felt stunned. Her daughter, her little girl, and she hadn't had the faintest idea. 'How are her studies going?'

'Very well. She'll get excellent grades, no doubt about that. Maths seems to be her best subject; maths and physics. When I phoned they said you were the council's chief quantity surveyor.'

Emma nodded.

Sister Annunciata laughed. 'That'll be where she gets it from then, all that calculating and measuring and scheduling.'

'What do you suggest I do, Sister?'

'The idea of her becoming a nun doesn't upset you?'

'No, not at all. I'm shocked, but . . .' Emma was lying. It was the last thing she'd have wanted for Ruth. The whole idea was repugnant to her.

'Then I suggest we simply do nothing. I don't think we should even tell her we've had this conversation. We'll keep it to ourselves and see how things develop. I felt I had to put you in the picture, though.'

'Thank you . . . thank you, Sister,' Emma faltered, struggling to get to grips with it all. 'If she did decide to become a nun, when would she have to commit herself?'

'Not for ages. We're a teaching order. She'd have to get her degree and a teaching qualification and then she'd take her vows if she still felt she had a vocation. But she could enter the convent and be with us while she studied, if she wished.'

Emma glanced at her watch. 'I have to get back, Sister.'

The nun followed her out of the sunlit room, and they walked down a long corridor with a terrazzo floor that led to the entrance hall. Every surface and every object in the bare uncluttered interior was scrubbed or dusted and polished. When Sister Annunciata opened a big oak door sunlight, humid warmth and birdsong invaded the cool silence.

'Thank you for coming, Mrs Turner.' The old nun took her hand and held it in both of hers. 'You have a wonderfully gifted daughter. We'll watch over her together, shall we?'

'Of course. Thank you, Sister.'

'And we'll not be saying a word?'

'Best not,' agreed Emma. Then she pulled her hand free and crunched across the gravel to her car.

*   *   *

By the time Emma got back to the office she'd decided not to tell her husband, Adam. If he could just bugger off and leave them, whatever the reason, he could wait for Ruth to tell him.

The phone began to ring. She picked up the handset and muttered, 'Emma Turner.'

'Emma, thank God. I've been trying to get hold of you for days; weeks in fact.'

'Who is this?' Emma knew very well who it was.

'It's Hugh; Hugh Dixon. Christ, don't pretend you don't know me.'

'Barfield Bricks,' Emma said, faking it for the switch board operator. 'The problem with the quote for the red rustics.'

He got the message. 'That's right. We can't

hold it much longer. I must meet you so we can discuss it.'

'It's difficult,' Emma said. 'My diary's full and . . .'

'I have to resolve the problem. Things will be impossible for me if I don't. Could I talk to you over lunch tomorrow? You must eat sometime,' he insisted. 'How about the Red Lion?'

Emma chewed her lip. She had to nip this in the bud. She was becoming a little scared at the way he was pestering her. The best thing would be to meet him and make it clear she couldn't have anything more to do with him. 'OK, but it'll have to be brief, and not the Red Lion. I'll meet you in the Horse and Groom at one on Wednesday.'

'That's next week.'

'It's the best I can do.'

'How about tonight?'

'Absolutely out of the question.'

'Next Wednesday, then.' He sounded bitterly disappointed. 'So long as you realize things are pretty desperate with me.'

CHAPTER THREE

Samantha Quest allowed her gaze to wander idly over whitewashed breeze-block walls, a concrete floor, and dirty windows that looked over an expanse of grass where a motor mower was sending up a cloud of clippings.

Thirteen men were sitting on cheap wooden chairs that had been arranged to face the battered table they'd given her for a desk. She recognized a local solicitor, the owner of a used car showroom, the manager of the town's only department store, and a financial adviser. The rest, she surmised, were probably in business in a modest way.

The men were looking her over with much more than interest. Legs crossed, she was gently swinging a foot from which dangled a strappy Jimmy Choo sandal with a stiletto heel. A couple of heads on the front row were nodding with the motion; others were trying to get a glimpse of stocking-covered thigh above the hem of her white summer dress. Who'd said rugby was a game for ruffians played by gentlemen? Like most aphorisms, she mused, it was witty rather than accurate.

'We're just waiting for Andrew and James now.' Jack Walters, one of the players who'd hired her, offered that.

A man sitting close to her table said, 'You're not from round these parts, are you petal?' He was six-six tall and broad as a barn door.

Samantha shook her head. 'From London.'

'Lasses in London, are they all as gorgeous as you?' Samantha turned down the corners of her mouth to kill the smile. The slightest encouragement and they'd get completely out of hand. 'I wouldn't rate a second glance in London,' she said huskily.

'All shirt lifters, are they love, blokes in London?'

'Second glance! I can't take my eyes off you,' came a voice from the back.

'You'll go blind if you're not careful, William,' cackled another voice.

Others joined in, the comments becoming more ribald. Being in a gang gave them confidence. If they were alone with her she'd soon have them red-faced and tongue-tied.

The talk and laughter were getting louder. Johnson, the other of the two players who'd hired her, stood up and yelled, 'Lads, lads, let's have a bit of quiet. This is serious business. We're not going to be talking about missing trophies. This is closer to home.' He glanced towards the door. Two youngish men in tracksuits were sidling in. 'About time. Get sat down, you two. We've been waiting ages.'

When the din had subsided he smiled down at Samantha, then turned to the team and said, 'I'm going to let Miss Quest, Miss Samantha Quest, tell you what this is all about. It's not pleasant and it's very personal: personal to each and every one of us. She wanted to talk to everyone individually, but I told her we play together, scrum down together, take a bath together after the match. We've no secrets. We're bonded. And doing it this way saves time and money.' He smiled at Samantha again, then sat down and said gently, 'You go ahead, love'.

Samantha glanced at the papers on the battered table. The team, the Barfield Barbarians, weren't laughing now. Their frowning faces were beginning to display concern as well as curiosity. She'd already decided not to spare their feelings, to tell it how it was.

'Mr Walters and Mr Johnson hired me a week ago to investigate whether or not some of your wives are using a male prostitute; a gigolo. Mr Walters had overheard telephone conversations between his wife and the wives of other team members, and when he conferred with Mr Johnson, Mr Johnson discovered an advertisement for an escort agency and an incriminating photograph in his wife's handbag. That's when they decided to call me in.'

She paused and looked across at them, then added, 'Now you know what this is about, some of you may be unhappy with the way I'm giving my report. If anyone would like me to talk to him privately, he ought to say so now.'

A chair creaked, breaking the silence, and a giant with tree-trunk thighs said, 'Keep going love. As far as I'm concerned we can hear it together. Just get it over with.'

Samantha waited a few seconds, then asked, 'Are you all OK with that?'

She let her gaze wander over tense faces,

scowling faces, faces wide-eyed with disbelief. Taking the silence to signify their assent, she went on, 'I'm afraid my investigations have confirmed what Mr Walters and Mr Johnson feared. I'm able to tell you that the wives of thirteen of the fifteen team members have been using the services of the escort agency. Would you like me to identify the two men whose wives are not involved so you can ask them to leave?'

'What exactly are you able to tell us, Miss Quest?' The one she'd recognized as a local solicitor asked that.

'When Mr Walters and Mr Johnson engaged me they asked me, using their own words, "to uncover every sordid little detail", and I've proceeded on that basis.'

'And how sure are you of your facts?'

'Short of catching your wives in flagrante delicto, I can more or less guarantee the accuracy of the information I'm going to give you.'

'What's she mean, "In flagrante delicto"?' whispered a voice.

'Catching the buggers at it,' came a muttered reply.

'I don't see any point asking anyone to leave,' the solicitor went on. 'It seems we're damn near all affected.'

The silence in the shabby room was electrifying now; not a cough, a chair creak or even the sound of breathing disturbed it.

Fifteen pairs of eyes were locked on hers.

'Before I begin,' Samantha said, 'I should make it clear that if any of you try and resolve this with violence, I'll have no alternative but to hand the papers over to the police.' She paused at that. She was lying. She never kept any files or papers, and she knew the warning might do nothing to protect the women, but she had to try.

'All of the incidents involve the same man, a male prostitute, a gigolo, on the books of a London escort agency. His working name is James Noble, and I have some photographs.'

Samantha gathered up the half-dozen copies of a large glossy composite of the three shots she'd taken in the hotel, moved around the table and distributed them amongst the team.

Someone muttered, 'Look at the tackle on the scrawny bastard,' and Samantha began to hear muttered curses.

'Lads, there's a lady present. Save it for later,' Johnson protested, then gave Samantha a grim look and said, 'Just keep going, love.'

'He's thirty-three and highly educated. As you can see from the photographs, he's extremely handsome. He's also cultured and charming. The agency's rates vary, depending on whether the engagement is for an afternoon, an afternoon and an evening, or all through the night, but they average about fifty pounds an hour.'

'You mean he's been paid to poke my missus?'

'I'd want paying to poke your missus, Jeremy.'

There was some laughter, but most of the men were silent, their faces tense and deathly pale.

'In addition to the agency fee,' Samantha went on, 'the client would also have to pay for meals, drinks, hotel accommodation and any entertainment.'

She reached across the table for a folder and took out a schedule of names and dates she'd prepared by cross-referencing the gigolo's diary notes with the information he'd given her at gunpoint.

'Perhaps it would be best if I take the names in alphabetical order. The first is Abrahams, Mrs Jackie Abrahams. She spent the afternoons of the fourth of January and the tenth of February with Noble. She also spent the evening and night with him on the twenty-third and fourth of February.'

Samantha glanced up as she added, 'I'll be giving all of you information of this kind; it might be a good idea for you to jot it down so you can check it against bank statements, your own diaries or your wives' recollections later.'

She returned to the schedule. 'Mrs Abrahams's first two meetings with Noble took place at the Ambassador Hotel, the rest at the Majestic. They always dined in the hotel during the evening sessions, and on the twenty-third of February went to see a musical show called The Hot Kimono.'

Samantha glanced up. The solicitor's chin was trembling. She guessed he was called Abrahams.

'As I said,' she went on, 'I was instructed to uncover every sordid little detail, so I'll tell you that Mrs Abrahams had sex twice on each of the afternoon sessions, and several times during the all-night engagements. I can supply more information than that, but I imagine it's as much detail as you require.'

'How did you find this out?' the solicitor demanded. 'If you know all this, who else does? And how could you identify my wife? I wasn't asked for a photograph.'

Samantha looked at him across the battered table. His putty-coloured face was crumpling; he was losing control. He suddenly jerked to his feet and made for the door but hands held on to him and drew him back.

'Let's hear it all, Jim. Then we'll have a talk and leave together. It's no good you dashing off and telling your missus and her warning the rest before we've a chance to get home.'

The solicitor sank back into his seat and put his face in his hands.

'How I got the information is very much my business,' Samantha said. 'The only people who have it are you, me, your wives and the prostitute; and my discretion is absolute. Mr

Walters and Mr Johnson supplied photographs of their wives; the rest were professionally done enlargements of faces in a group picture taken at your last Christmas party.'

'Can we get on?' a voice demanded irritably.

Samantha looked down at the schedule. 'Julie Baxter is next.'

There were no more interruptions. She occasionally heard a muffled curse and the words bitch and slag floated around the room, but they let her deliver her report on their wives and partners.

'If a woman's not been mentioned, does it mean she's not been fooling around?' The man who asked that was standing at the back of the room: black curly hair just turning grey, handsome outdoor face, tall and powerfully built; his body hadn't succumbed to the paunchiness displayed by some of the younger men.

'It means she wasn't involved with this particular prostitute. As you'll have gathered, the ladies I've mentioned were probably recommending him to one another. My instructions confined me to investigating that situation.'

'How did they pay?' a voice asked.

'The agency accepts cash or credit cards and payment has to be made at the time of the booking. Cards presented by women are charged to an account called Regal Fabrics and Soft Furnishings. The agency is obviously doing its best to be discreet.'

'And how much has it cost us to find all this out?'

'It might be better if we'd not,' another player muttered.

'I've already paid Miss Quest,' Jack Walters said. 'We might not like what she's told us, but she's done a thorough job and she's done it quick. I reckon what she's charged is reasonable and not a lot when it's shared fifteen ways. We can talk about that later. It's no use wishing you hadn't been told. A man needs to know if his wife's messing about behind his back, especially if it's with some dirty sod from London.'

The atmosphere in the shabby room was sombre now, and the men were avoiding one another's eyes. Samantha dropped the file of papers into her attaché case, clicked it shut and rose to her feet. 'If you've no more questions, gentlemen, I'll leave you to talk about this amongst yourselves. One last thing: I meant it when I said I'll forward the papers to the police if there's any violence.'

She swept past them, fragrant in a cloud of perfume, tall in the high-heeled sandals; the full skirt of her white Malandrino dress swirling around her knees. The men weren't ogling her now. Icy waters of betrayal had extinguished the fires of lust.

Leaving the meeting room, Samantha crossed a dusty bar area, pushed at the outer door, and emerged into the sunlight. She began to pick her way carefully; Jimmy Choos weren't made for walking over the clinker that bordered the pitch. When she reached the Ferrari, she tossed her attaché case into the back, slid inside and slammed the door, letting out a little sigh as the feel and fragrance of sun-warmed leather enveloped her.

Her mobile started cheeping. She groped for it in her bag.

'Sam Quest?'

'Speaking?'

'I'm Adam Turner. You don't know me but I was wondering if you could help me?'

'In what way would I be helping you, Mr Turner?'

'It's difficult over the phone.'

'It always is. Try,' she insisted.

'It's my daughter, Ruth. I'm worried about her. I think she may be in some sort of trouble.'

'And what kind of trouble do you think she might be in?'

'I think she might have been abused. Or somebody might be abusing her. Like I said, it's difficult over the phone. If I could come and see you ...'

'I'm not a social worker, Mr Turner. And I'm expensive.'

'And I'm a father who's left the marital home and I'm worried sick about my daughter.'

'I don't like time-wasters, Mr Turner.'

'At least let me come and see you. Even if you don't get involved I'll pay you for the talking time.'

Samantha sighed. 'It might be better if I come and see you. Where are you now?'

'At the shop, Fine Arts and Antiques, off the Leeds-Bradford Road, just outside Barfield.' His voice had brightened. He gave her the address.

'Is there anywhere to park?'

'The rear yard. Drive through the archway at the side of the pub, it's the Angel and Royal, and turn first left through the gateway.'

'I'll be there in fifteen minutes.'

As she drew the seat belt over, Samantha looked back at the ramshackle clubhouse. 'Barfield Barbarians' was spelt out in yellow plastic letters on a black fascia; yellow and black were the team's colours. She smiled to herself. Perhaps if they'd been a little less barbaric their wives wouldn't have found shared solace in the arms of the sensitive young gigolo.

CHAPTER FOUR

Betty Slater forked up the three-quarter-pound steak, turned it over and lowered it back into the sizzling fat. Jack would be home

47

soon. She could feel the tension rising in her, that tightening in her chest.

She poured frozen peas into a pan and turned up the gas, lifted the basket of chips from the fryer and rested it across the top to drain. She was praying there wouldn't be any trouble tonight. She couldn't cope with any more rows. Her nerves were shot to pieces. She couldn't stand him yelling at her with his mouth so close to her ear she could feel his breath and his spit on her cheek. He'd got worse, much worse, since he got the contract to supply big concrete blocks for that council job. He had to keep up a steady supply and he got really stressed out when things didn't go right at the plant.

She moved the steak with the fork, turned down the gas under the peas so they'd simmer. When she glanced at the clock she saw he was late and that made her uneasy. If he'd had problems he'd be in that truculent mood and she couldn't bear any more of his tight-lipped anger; the cold hate in his staring eyes.

She heard the slam of his van door. Her stomach began to churn and she tried to control the trembling of her hands as she forked the steak on to a plate and strained the peas. His heavy boots clumped down the side of the house, across the patio, and then he was coming into the kitchen.

'Your tea's ready, love.' She couldn't look at him. She shook the chips on to his plate and carried it over to the table. 'Steak and chips; is that okay?'

He flopped down into a chair and reached for the tomato sauce. Betty risked a glance. He was staring at her: not angry, just cold and distant.

She busied herself at the sink, stealing the occasional wary glance at his broad back, the mass of black curly hair. It was greying at the temples now, but he was still handsome, all hard muscle, not an ounce of fat on him. He was eating slowly. He usually made a ravenous assault on everything she gave him.

'Is it all right, love? There's nothing wrong, is there?'

'Come and sit down here, where I can see you.'

Betty went around the Formica table, drew out one of the tubular chrome chairs, and sat facing him. He forked a chunk of steak and some chips into his mouth, then looked up at her, alternately chewing and sucking in air to cool the hot food.

He swallowed noisily, then growled, 'Do you have much to do with the other wives at the club? You know, socialize, meet them in town and such like?'

Betty gave him a puzzled, fearful look. 'You know I don't, love. We've never had the money to keep up, not until this last couple of years. I mean, most of the blokes at the rugby club are solicitors and accountants and such like. And some of the wives have decent jobs themselves. It makes a difference.'

'Do you know a bloke called Noble?'

Betty shook her head; looked blank.

'The other wives; they ever talk to you about a bloke called Noble, James Noble?'

'I've told you, love, I never ever see them to talk to them about anything.' She nodded towards his plate. 'Your steak's going to get cold, love.'

'Where were you this morning?'

Betty's heart began to pound. When he started this questioning he was always in one of his crazily jealous moods. 'I went to that antique shop I told you about. There's a lovely little gilded desk I fancy for the bedroom. I went in to ask how much it was.'

'You were in the shop a long time. And you've been there before.'

'How do you know I . . .'

'Never you mind how I know. What's he like, this bloke in the shop?'

The ice was getting very thin now. She'd have to be careful what she said. 'He's just a middle-aged man. He seems to know a lot about antiques. He does the restoration himself.'

'What's he look like?'

Betty shrugged. 'Tall, fair-haired, a bit on the thin side, middle-aged. I was more interested in the desk, love. I didn't take a lot of notice.'

'Business must do well. He lives along Auckland Crescent; number sixty-five.'

'How do you know that? I didn't know.'

'I know a lot of things.' He was staring at her with cold, dead eyes, his lips pressed into an angry line.

God, she must have been brain dead. She should have listened to her gran. But you just talk when you're sixteen. You don't do a lot of listening. All she'd wanted was Jack kissing her, his big hands roaming all over her. He was big and handsome even then: he'd looked like a man when he wasn't much more than a boy. She'd lived off the buzz it gave her, the other boys too scared to come near her, the girls all sick with envy. She'd felt wanted, protected. Sweet Jesus, she'd soon found out what protected meant. She had the scars to prove it.

'Fancy him, do you?' He turned the words into a sneer.

She laughed. 'Course I don't fancy him.'

His face darkened. Laughing had been a mistake. 'Then what were you doing all that time in the shop with the poncey git?'

'He was just showing me the desk, love.'

Jack Slater suddenly lunged across the table and grabbed her hair.

'Get off me,' she screamed. 'Get off me.'

'And what were you showing him?' He tore open the bodice of her dress. 'Were you showing him these?'

Shoving the flimsy table aside, he dragged

51

her to her feet. 'You were in the shop with him for half an hour. Half a bloody hour.' His fingers were combed into her hair, twisting it painfully, and he was holding her close, yelling the words into her ear.

'The man was showing me the desk. That's all it was, Jack. He's restoring it, fixing the drawers and putting new leather on the top. Don't, Jack.' She was screaming with the pain. 'Don't Jack. Don't . . .'

He dragged her out of the kitchen, across the hall and into the sitting room; forced her on to her knees in front of the sofa, then hurled her face into the cushions.

'No, Jack, please . . .' Her screams were muffled by the fabric now.

'If you so much as let the bastard touch you, you're dead. I'll kill him, and then I'll kill you.' He shook her head. 'Can you hear me?'

She felt his huge thigh thrusting between her legs, pressing her against the sofa. She tensed. She knew what was coming.

'Can you fucking hear me?' He tugged at her hair.

'Yes, Jack. Please, Jack . . .'

'His fist thudded into her side, just above the waist, driving upwards, forcing all the breath out of her.

'You're dead, you big fat cow. You're bloody dead.'

She tried to draw breath through the cushions, tried to tense herself for the next blow. And then, through the red darkness, she heard the phone ringing.

He wrenched her head back, then threw it down into the cushions as he scrambled to his feet. She listened to the tread of his boots, then his gravelly voice reciting his name into the phone in the hall. She forced herself to her feet, crept past him and began to pull herself up the stairs. She stopped on the half-landing, dragging in shallow breaths, fighting to control the pain in her side.

'How many did you say you were sending?'

'Three! I've told you, the blocks can only take two. They're not big enough for any more chambers.'

She caught the faint sound of an agitated voice at the other end of the line.

'Small? Small won't make any difference. Tell Vrakimi this is his problem. Just bring two. There'll be another block ready early Thursday morning. Tell him it's the best I can do.'

There was a silence, then he snarled, 'I don't think you understand the English language, old son. Two, not three, and they don't come until after midnight. Have you got that?'

The phone crashed down. Betty heard him stamp back into the sitting room, then retrace his steps to the hall, as she struggled up the last flight of stairs.

'Betty!' he yelled up at her. 'Betty! I've to go

to the works. I'll be back late. Don't go out of this house. Do you hear me? And you're not having the desk so you've no need to go back to that poncey shop.'

The door slammed, she listened to the tread of his boots down the path, the whine of a starter, then the rumble of his truck, fading as he drove away.

She sat on the edge of the bath for a while, her hands on her knees, rocking herself. After what seemed like an age, some paracetamol she'd taken began to ease the pain. She stood up and started to undress while the bath filled.

Frightened blue eyes stared back at her out of the mirror. Her copper-blonde hair had been tangled by Jack's rough handling and crying had made her face puffy and blotchy. She'd got a figure, but she wasn't fat. And she hadn't put on that much weight since she was a girl. She could still get into a size fourteen. Well, she could if it wasn't skimped. She emptied half a packet of Radox into the bath, stirred it with the back scrubber and lowered herself in.

Jack was an utter pig. She couldn't go on. He seemed to be in this crazy, jealous mood all the time now. He was obviously watching her. He'd probably been sitting in his van while she went into that shop. If she could be sure he'd never find out, she'd have a revenge fling, have the secret satisfaction of knowing she'd done the very thing that would hurt him most.

Strange Jack should be so upset about the bloke in the antique shop, because he *had* fancied her. She could tell that by the way she'd caught him gazing at her when he thought she wasn't looking.

Betty began to sob. Calling her a fat cow! If it wasn't for the house she'd leave him. She'd spent ten years getting it the way it was, sewing curtains, decorating, scrimping and scraping. Thank God they hadn't had any kids. She tried to stop sobbing. It only sent the pain stabbing through her. She lifted her arm and peered at the red mark that would be a black bruise tomorrow. Perhaps he'd cracked her ribs. The pig! She wished she'd never have to hear his feet clumping down the path again.

*　　*　　*

Samantha Quest swung the silver Ferrari Modena beneath the archway at the side of the Angel and Royal. Emerging at the rear, she made a sharp left into a cobbled yard and climbed out of the car. She picked her way across the uneven stones, then walked back, under the archway, to the front of the shop. It was artfully tricked out in grey and gold, and there were some choice pieces of antique furniture in the window. She pushed at a shiny black door and set bells jangling as she stepped inside.

A tallish, wiry man in an open-necked shirt

emerged from an opening at the rear and moved towards her through the furniture. 'Can I help you?' His pleasant smile transformed uneven masculine features, made them almost attractive. His shirt and jeans, even his carpenter's apron, looked clean and freshly ironed.

'Mr Turner?'

'That's right.'

'I'm Samantha Quest. You phoned me.' She didn't offer her hand, just stood there looking him over.

Bushy eyebrows lifted. 'Forgive me, I thought Sam Quest was a man.'

Samantha slid her sunglasses down to the tip of her nose and treated him to the vivid blaze of her emerald green eyes. 'Do I look like a man?' she asked huskily.

He let out an embarrassed laugh. 'Forgive me, no. I've never seen a woman who looked less like a man, but . . .'

'But I sound like one, is that it?'

'Not when we're face to face.' He was becoming flustered. 'But over the telephone . . .' He gestured towards the rear of the shop. 'Please, come through. We can talk better in the workshop.' He moved around her, locked the shop door, turned a card to 'Closed', then followed her into the back.

He tugged a dustsheet from an ornate white and gold chair. 'Sit on this. It's just been re-covered. It won't mark your dress.'

Samantha reclined back and laid her bare arms along the arms of the chair.

'Can I get you some tea or coffee? I've no alcohol here.'

'Tea would be good.'

'Earl Grey with lemon?'

'That would be perfect.' She was warming to him.

She let her gaze wander around the workshop while he put a kettle on an old gas ring he used for boiling glue. Two rooms had been knocked into one at the back of the shop. A workbench was arranged along one wall; above it, tools were hanging neatly from long racks. In the middle of the floor, a big low table had been covered with carpet to protect furniture laid out on it for repair. The walls were freshly emulsioned cream, the concrete floor painted a dull tile red. Sunlight was streaming through windows set high in two of the walls. It was as clean as an operating theatre: a place for everything and everything in its place. Samantha thought the extreme tidiness verged on the obsessional.

He brought her tea in a large but delicate china cup. 'Hope this is OK.'

She took a sip. 'It's perfect. Thanks.'

'The chair suits you.'

She raised an eyebrow.

'A beautiful woman in a beautiful Malandrino dress in a beautiful French chair.'

Samantha removed her sunglasses and slid

them into her bag. 'You can recognize a Malandrino dress?'

'Courrèges, Donatella Versace, Catherine Malandrino, Dior, Chanel. I used to work for Manson and Lane, the big advertising agency in Leeds; we did a lot of publicity spreads for the fashion houses.' He perched on the low carpet-covered table, sipped at the aromatic tea, and looked across at her.

Samantha didn't speak, just gazed back.

The silence soon embarrassed him, so he gabbled on, 'Studied at the Slade. I was good at figure drawing and illustration work. Drawing beautiful women in beautiful clothes was a pleasant change from refrigerators and car engines.'

'You gave it up?'

'It more or less dried up. Got made redundant from Manson and Lane; got a lecturer's job at the local art college and got made redundant from that. Decided I'd be better off employing myself.' He gave a wry grin and added, 'So, here I am.'

Samantha sipped the tea. It was cooling now and the infusion of lemon was making it refreshing. She went on gazing at him without speaking. He seemed a good-natured and decent man, trying to fight off defeat when he should have been enjoying some success in his middle years.

'You said you were worried about your daughter.'

'I'm worried sick.'

'How old is she?'

'Seventeen, almost eighteen. Goes to St Mary's, the Roman Catholic girls' school.'

'And what makes you think something's wrong?'

'I left my wife, just after Christmas. I live above the shop now. Ruth, that's my daughter, was OK at first. Our splitting up didn't seem to affect her. She'd always been close to her mother, and I'd been away a lot the previous year buying and selling and getting some decent pieces together for this place. And she only lives a mile away. She can come and see me whenever she wants.'

He paused, looked down at his hands, then spoke more slowly as he went on, 'It was about three months ago that I sensed a change. She began to come here much more often and she seemed more affectionate. She even stayed the night here a couple of times when her mother was away. Her mother's the council's chief quantity surveyor and she sometimes has to go to seminars, conferences, that sort of thing. Before, she'd have stayed at her best friend's.'

Samantha slid her empty cup on to the carpet-covered table. 'That doesn't amount to anything, Mr Turner. You could have expected much more trouble after parting from your wife.'

He glanced up. 'There's more. I was just giving you the background. About a couple of months ago, right out of the blue, she asked me if people were always rough and coarse when they had sex.' He gave Samantha an embarrassed grin. 'I didn't know what to say. I mean, what sort of a question's that for a seventeen-year-old convent girl to ask her father?'

Samantha looked at the middle-aged man in a carpenter's apron sitting hunched with embarrassment on the table. He suddenly reached for his cup and drained the last of the tea, obviously trying to avoid her gaze. She said nothing, just watched and waited.

Presently he said, 'I told her sex was a very personal thing and asked her if she was in any kind of trouble; if some boy was bothering her, being unpleasant. She said there was nothing like that. Then, about a week ago, she phoned me one afternoon and said there was something she wanted to tell me and hoped I wouldn't be too upset. Then she went off somewhere with the school for a couple of days, and when she got back she said she didn't want to talk about it. What was I supposed to make of that?'

'Have you spoken to your wife?'

'Only once. She just laughed and said Ruth was fine. She said she didn't know what I was worrying about.'

'She could be right.'

He managed to meet her gaze. 'Like I told you on the phone, Miss Quest, I'm worried sick about her. One minute she's talking to me about rough sex, the next she wants to talk to me about something that's going to upset me and then she changes her mind.'

'What exactly do you want me to do?' Samantha asked. 'Watch her. See if she's involved in anything or with someone strange.' He gave a helpless little shrug. 'Just find out what you can about it all.'

'And who gave you my number?'

'Jack Walters. He's my accountant. We went to school together. He knows I've parted from my wife. I told him I was worried about Ruth being mixed up with some unpleasant little toe-rag and that I felt guilty about not being in the house for her. He suggested that I hire you. He said you'd just done a job for a friend of his.'

Samantha smiled to herself. Jack Walters was one of the rugby players who'd hired her to check on the gigolo. It was always a friend, never themselves, who'd needed an investigator.

'I'm expensive, Mr Turner.'

He laughed wryly. 'Jack said you were bloody expensive but you got results fast, so it was probably cheaper in the end.'

'All the same, isn't this something you and your wife could sort out yourselves?'

'I don't think so. She'd just laugh and tell me to stop worrying.'

Samantha went on looking at him. He met

her gaze for a while, smiling expectantly, then he looked down at his hands. She slowly uncrossed and re-crossed her legs, watched his eyes flick up to capture the movement. Then she asked, 'Why did you leave your wife?'

'Is that relevant?'

'It could be. Is there another man in the house now?'

'It was nothing like that. There's no one else involved. I just cleared out because I'd been unhappy with things for a long time.'

Samantha raised an eyebrow. 'Things?' she repeated huskily.

'I don't find it easy to talk about, even to Emma; that's my wife. I wouldn't know how to start explaining it to you.'

'Just try,' she said. 'It could hold the answer.'

He seemed exasperated. 'It's not easy. I'd need all day. I can't say it in a few words.'

'Try,' Samantha urged.

'Well, we just ended up being like brother and sister. I suppose I first noticed what had happened when I was made redundant. You have more time to think; you begin to realize what's going on around you. Emma just wasn't interested any more. I tried talking about it, joking about it, even getting angry about it, but she just evaded the issue. She didn't even like me touching her. Trouble is, I really love her and I fancy her something rotten; she's a very attractive woman. The whole situation was winding me up. I felt bloody humiliated; sick of the rejection and the endless frustration. I just cleared out in the end.'

'And you're sure there's no other man?'

He laughed bitterly. 'There couldn't be. She's not interested. She's just a workaholic. Her job's an all-consuming passion.'

Samantha gazed at him from under long lashes heavy with mascara. The ultimate delusion of the trusting husband: his wife wasn't interested in sex with him so she couldn't possibly be interested in sex with anyone else.

'I charge for a full week when I take on a case, Mr Turner. After that I charge by the hour. If it only takes me a day, you still pay for the full week,' Samantha said, then quoted the weekly and hourly rates.

He gave her a bleak smile. 'That's OK. I just want this dealing with. When will you start?'

'When is she next coming here to see you?'

'Saturday morning. I promised I'd go shopping with her and buy her something to wear for the end of term party. They invite the sixth form boys over from another school.'

'What time will she be here?'

'About ten.'

'I'll be here when she arrives. You tell her you've been called away and I'll offer to take her instead.'

'Aren't you going to watch her; to stake her out?'

Samantha laughed as she rose to her feet. 'I don't think your daughter would care to be staked out, Mr Turner, and watching her would take too long and probably get us nowhere. If I spend a day with her I'm pretty sure I'll find out what you want to know.' She moved back into the shop and headed for the door. 'Anyway, she'll get a much better party frock if she comes shopping with me.'

He unlocked the shop door and opened it for her, set the bells jangling at the back. 'Until Saturday, then.'

CHAPTER FIVE

Samantha Quest reversed the Ferrari into her tiny garage and lowered the window. Plugging one end of a cable into a pocket computer, the other into a socket on the wall, she began to scroll through images on the screen. Garage and utilities on the ground floor, kitchen and sitting room on the first floor, two bedrooms and a bathroom on the second. It was deserted. The uncluttered interior was just as she'd left it ten hours earlier. Her fingers flicked over the keys, interrogating the system, confirming that no one had violated her home.

Using the remote, she closed the up and over door, then went from garage to tiny hall and climbed stairs to the first floor.

Town houses; that's how the agents had described the tiny, three-storey dwellings built on a plot once occupied by a big detached house in the best part of Barfield. They'd been snapped up by young professionals and managers, mostly singles and couples: the houses were too small for families. It was anonymous. The residents came and went without intruding into one another's lives. When she'd passed the end of the tiny cul-de-sac on her drive north from London she'd known instinctively that she could lose herself here, fade into the background in this quiet respectable suburb of a small backwater town. She'd bought the furnished show house, the last dwelling to be sold. White woodwork, magnolia walls, beige carpets wall-to-wall and on every floor; the decor was comfortingly nondescript.

Samantha threw her bag on to the leather Habitat sofa, kicked off the Jimmy Choos, then headed up the next flight of stairs and padded into the main bedroom. From its window she could view the entire cul-de-sac, watch movements in and out and the traffic along the main Barfield road. She put her dress on a hanger, then decided to go back down and get a drink before taking a shower.

Her mobile was cheeping in her bag when she entered the sitting room. She took it out.

'That you, Peaches?'

'How did you get this number? And don't

call me Peaches.' It was all she needed. A call from this arrogant, related-to-royalty arsehole could only mean problems.

'Have you heard?'

'Heard what? Don't fool around, Marcus. I've just got in, I'm tired and I need a drink.'

'Switch on the television. The news is breaking on all channels.'

Samantha reached for the remote, keyed it and watched the image roll on to the screen: ambulances, firefighters, noise, chaos, and oily smoke oozing out of the entrance to what looked like a tube station.

'See it?'

'I can see it,' she muttered.

'Tottenham Court Road. They've finally done it. We thought we had the situation covered. Christ, there's going to be some monumental arse kickings over this.'

'How did they do it?'

'Not sure yet, but the explosion was on the south-bound train, just before it reached the platform. The tunnel roof's down. Rear carriages are cut off by debris.'

'Suicide bombers?'

'Could be, or they could be leaving packages. Whatever it is, they're using something stronger than Semtex. And that's not all. They bombed the Finsbury Park synagogue; wrecked the place.'

'How are you responding?'

'We've got our people in the crowd and all

over the central tube network. We've already started pulling in likely and not so likely suspects, nationwide. Things are difficult enough as it is; this could really destabilize things.'

Samantha watched the first of the stretchers being lifted into the convoy of ambulances. Black-helmeted, black-uniformed men, clutching assault rifles, were sealing off the street.

'We may have to call you in, Peaches.'

'I was promised out until what was left of the Berlin group had been dealt with. Everyone agreed it was too dangerous . . .'

'Al-Halabi and Mosharif are dead. A couple of CIA agents shot them in Alaska when they found them sussing out the oil pipelines. Agents didn't want the bother of all the extradition nonsense.'

'How do I know they're dead?'

'We've got a DNA match on both. They're dead. I'll send you the print-outs if you don't believe me.'

'You'd send me the match from a monkey and his uncle,' Samantha said bitterly. 'And it still leaves the American national, Nasari. He always worried me most.'

'The Russians are holding him somewhere in Siberia. Found him in Chechnya of all places. He's an embarrassment. They want him dead more than you do, but the Americans know they've got him and they're

67

claiming him back.'

'You can't expect me to go active with him still around.'

'He's in some ghastly gulag. He's not getting around.'

'Forget it,' Samantha protested. 'The deal was me out until the Berlin group had been eliminated.'

'What about Queen and country?'

'Sod Queen and country.'

'My, we are flashing our sharp little republican claws.'

'And don't you dare remind me you're ninety-ninth in line to the bloody throne, Marcus. It's more than I could bear.'

Samantha heard him laughing down the line. 'The glass ceilings are going, Peaches. Women are running it all now: Flying Squad, Special Branch, MI5. Another five years and you could be at the top.'

'Yeah, surrounded by sycophantic pricks who call me ma'm to my face and Peaches behind my back.'

There was some more laughter, then the ultra-refined voice became serious. 'We may have no alternative but to call you in. Stay where I can reach you. I'll get back to you in a couple of days.'

Samantha switched off the phone. The news broadcast had moved to the Finsbury Park synagogue. Its walls were still standing but the roof had gone and the interior was a smouldering, fire-damaged ruin.

She went over to a small drinks table; that and a document shredder, the sofa and the television, were the only items in the room. She poured a large measure of scotch, then padded through to the kitchen and splashed a little tap water into the glass. Sipping the drink, she continued to watch the newscast.

It all seemed remote and unreal, a million miles from her hideaway in this nondescript little Yorkshire town. The two years she'd spent here had had a healing effect. There were nights now when she didn't wake up moaning with her body drenched in sweat. She didn't want to go back. Marcus had promised her. He should hand out guns to the politicians: they'd allowed the country to get into this God-awful mess.

*   *   *

Jack Slater tugged the release chain and cement poured in a dusty grey cloud from the hopper into the rotating drum. It began to mix with the gravel, and the deafening rattle of stones on steel was muffled a little.

He looked down the production line. The new blokes had done a good job of assembling the reinforcement for tomorrow's block. The network of bars, tied together with wire, rose like a huge cage, half way up to the roof. One block ready for shuttering by the men tomorrow, one block cast and waiting for the shuttering to be struck, and one block steam cured and ready to be delivered to site.

Betty was a lying bitch. She'd been to that antique place three times and yesterday she'd stayed more than half an hour. Bloody desk! What did the stupid cow want with a desk? Somewhere to write a note to the milkman? Somewhere to write little love notes to the bugger in the shop, more likely.

It was good of old Frank to tip him off. Good of him to keep the street surveillance cameras pointing towards the shop. Frank understood. He knew the score: copper on night duty who'd come home to find his missus in bed with a brother officer. Bitches; you can't trust 'em.

Jack went into the storeroom, measured out chemicals to speed up the set and make the concrete flow more quickly, then carried the plastic container to the water tank and poured in the pungent smelling mixture. He had to have a rapid set. The concrete in the shafts that penetrated deep into the blocks needed to be rock-hard by morning.

The sound of an engine was audible now, despite the rumble and clatter of the giant concrete mixer. He strode over to a tall metal door and slid it aside. A battered white van began to reverse into the factory.

While Jack was heaving the door shut and securing it, the swarthy black-haired driver climbed out of the cab. 'Vrakimi's not a happy man,' he yelled, over the din.

'What do you mean, he's not a happy man?' Jack demanded. The cold-eyed arrogance of the Albanian angered him.

'If he says you take three, he expects you to take three. He told me to remind you of all the money he's paid you.'

Jack Slater glared down at the man, fists clenched, speechless with rage. The Albanian ignored him, opened the van doors and began to throw old cardboard fruit crates towards the cab. Jack grabbed him by the shoulder, turned him to face the production line. 'Look,' he ranted, struggling to form a coherent sentence, 'Three blocks: one ready for shuttering, one poured, one ready to go. Every night I get one block I can put them in. One bloody block, savvy?' He was yelling the words in the man's ear. 'In one block I can form two compartments. Three into flicking two won't go. It might do in Albania, but not in Britain. Understand?'

The driver shook his shoulder free and flicked at his jacket with fingers tufted with black hair. 'I understand,' he snapped. 'I'm not stupid. But Vrakimi's not happy.'

He stared up at Jack, loathing etched into his face. When the contract was over, when this English pig could provide no more hiding places, he'd deal with him.

He turned, threw the rest of the cardboard

trays on to the heap behind the cab, then dragged a black-polythene wrapped bundle half out of the van. He glanced at Jack, and together they lifted it down on to the factory floor. After they'd lifted out the second bundle, he slammed the van doors, pushed past Jack and climbed back into the cab.

Jack Slater followed and grabbed the edge of the door to stop him pulling it shut. 'Haven't you forgotten something?'

Contempt glittered in the little Albanian's eyes. He reached inside his jacket, tugged out a grubby envelope and tossed it down.

Jack opened the flap and laboriously thumbed through the bundle of notes. When he was sure it was all there, he slid back the factory door and the van coughed into life and lurched past him into the darkness.

Jack studied his watch. He had to be careful. Having added so much accelerator the concrete would harden in the mixer if he left it churning too long. He switched on the pumps and water and chemicals began to splash into the rotating drum.

He returned to the store room at the back of the office, took a face mask and pressed it from its blister pack, then picked a pair of surgical gloves from an opened box and drew them on.

Only God knew what the filthy slags were infected with. They came wrapped in black plastic bin liners, one drawn down over the

72

head, the other pulled up from the feet. When fetid air escaped from the wrappings the smell was sickening. It was unlike anything he'd ever encountered: a mixture of vomit and ordure and, occasionally, something like chickens, freshly plucked and drawn.

Jack dragged the larger of the two bundles into the centre of the floor and laid it alongside a heavy steel reinforcing bar. Keeping the turns of tape close and tight, he began to bind corpse to bar until it took on the appearance of a bandaged mummy.

He'd made a mess of his first interment. He'd only bound the corpse in a couple of places and it had sagged into a crouching position on the bar. Bile rose in his throat every time he recalled the way he'd struggled to force the stinking bundle down the narrow shaft in the concrete block.

He pressed a switch mounted on one of the steel columns and a crane rumbled towards him along a gantry. When it was overhead he lowered the hook, attached it to a ring formed at the top of the reinforcing bar, and hoisted the corpse into the air. Jack manoeuvred it over the concrete block, then lowered it into the narrow shaft.

When he dragged the smaller bundle over, the bin liners parted, exposing the body of a young girl. Not much more than a child, her flat chest was covered by a skimpy cotton blouse. The lower half of her body was naked,

73

the dead grey flesh taking on a yellowish-green tinge where it stretched tight over angular hips. Jack's gaze rested for a few seconds on the tiny mound of ginger pubic hair, then he dragged the polythene back and began to bind her body to the bar.

Just a kid, he muttered, pulling the tape savagely tight. Stupid little tart should have done what she was told, worked off the cost of getting her into the country, clothing her, feeding her, providing her with a room and a bed.

Vrakimi had told him the women ended up dead because they got awkward, started to get choosy about clients, tried to break his hold on them, even tried to go to the police for help. When that happened, the unruly ones had to be dealt with or they'd all get out of hand.

Jack used the overhead crane to lower the corpse into the shaft, then climbed a ladder to the top of the block. He swung a chute over, positioned its outlet above the first of the two holes, then threw a lever that tilted the rotating drum. Lumpy grey sludge flowed from drum to chute and began to pour down the shaft. He shook the bar holding the corpse, trying to make the gruel-like mixture fill every void and cavity, then he repeatedly plunged a long rod down the gaps around the body, tamping the concrete down.

When the first chamber had been filled, he dragged the chute over and repeated the process with the second, sealing in the scrawny, child-like body. His judgement had been perfect: there was just enough mixture to fill the spaces. He climbed down, turned on a pump that sent water cascading into the drum and along the chute, washing away the remains of the grey slurry, leaving everything clean for the men when they arrived later that morning.

Jack took a trowel to the top of the block, worked at the hardening mixture until it was smooth and indistinguishable from the rest of the concrete. The chemicals accelerating the set had made it warm, almost hot. Another day and the block would be ready for delivery to the site.

*   *   *

Jack Slater drove up the rise and past the school. He'd finished earlier than he'd expected. Apart from the stupid Albanian, he'd had no problems and there was an envelope stuffed with twenties in his pocket. He made more out of Vrakimi than the entire gang did during the day and the taxman didn't see a penny of it. And there seemed to be a steady supply of prossies. Vrakimi had told him they were brought from London, Manchester, Leeds: most of the big cities. Trouble was, he didn't have an endless supply of holes in concrete blocks and he was already halfway through the contract. It was a case of

75

making hay while the sun shone.

Heading down an unlit dip in the road, Jack switched the headlights to full beam. He saw him then, way up ahead, a jogger in a white T-shirt and shorts, his white ankle socks flitting backwards and forwards like moths in the beam of light. Jogging at one in the morning; must be keen! Jack realized then that he'd seen him before. Whenever he'd travelled home at this time he'd passed him on this unlit stretch of road that ran between open fields. The van was closing on the runner. It was him: close-cropped blond hair, tall, athletic build.

Immersed in thought, the man didn't even glance over his shoulder as the van swept past.

CHAPTER SIX

Samantha Quest pushed at the shiny black door and set the bell jangling as she stepped into the antique shop. It wasn't ten yet, but the July sun was already warming the interior, and furniture closest to the window had been sheeted over to protect it from the glare.

Adam Turner was standing in the workshop doorway. He was still wearing jeans and an open-necked shirt, but he'd discarded the joiner's apron. He smiled at her as she made her way through the furniture towards him. When she got closer he said, 'No Catherine

Malandrino today?' He pondered, then said, 'Looks like Dior.'

Samantha laughed. 'Chloë. You're not infallible, Mr Turner.'

He gave her a wry smile. 'I was guessing. I'd really no idea. I'm too old and too out-of-touch, that's the trouble.' His gaze wandered appreciatively over the sleeveless saffron dress with its bootlace straps, then moved on to her Gucci shoes and handbag.

'Your daughter's not arrived?' Samantha asked.

'No. She's due around ten. I've arranged for the phone people to send me an alarm call at quarter past. I thought it would make it seem more convincing when I tell her the trip's off. Who shall I say you are?'

'May as well use my real name. Why not say I'm an interior designer looking for pieces for a hotel refurbishment?'

He nodded. 'How about some tea while we're waiting?'

'Thanks, but no,' Samantha said. 'Perhaps you could show me some of these things. We ought to look as if we're doing business when she arrives.'

Adam Turner drew the dustsheets from the items close to the window and began to talk to her about the way the furniture was designed and constructed.

Samantha sensed he'd become immersed in his new business and picked up quite a lot in the year he'd spent getting the stock together. He tugged out drawers, turned items so they could view the backs, explained the features that dated them. She remained detached: veneer and banding and cabriole legs didn't do it for her. He became engrossed, trying his best to respond to her feigned interest.

The bell jangled. Adam Turner glanced up. 'Ruth! You OK?'

'Fine, Daddy, thanks.' The girl's voice was refined. Home and school had eliminated every trace of a Yorkshire accent.

Samantha turned, saw a young woman dressed in a grey pleated skirt, a white blouse, and a red blazer with green stripes. Her stockings were dark, her black shoes highly polished and serviceable. Unusual, Samantha thought, a seventeen-year-old wearing her school uniform on Saturday.

'This is Miss Quest. She's trying to find some pieces for a hotel refurbishment. Miss Quest, this is my daughter, Ruth.'

The girl said, 'Hullo.' She didn't offer her hand, but gave a polite smile that held no warmth. Tall, she had her father's blue eyes and blonde hair. The resemblance ended there. Another ten years and she'd be a very beautiful woman, Samantha thought.

The phone began to ring in the back room. Adam Turner grinned apologetically and said, 'Excuse me,' and went to answer it.

Ruth was looking Samantha over. Her

expression was wary. When their eyes met, Ruth said, 'It's going to be scorching.'

Samantha nodded. 'Your father's going to have to put the dustsheets back. He's got some very nice furniture here.'

'He buys and sells a lot of stuff, but only the best pieces end up in the shop. He does all the restoration himself. He's very good at it.' For the first time there was some animation in the girl's voice.

'You help him?'

Ruth laughed. 'Not really. I'm hopeless at that sort of thing. I've done a bit of dusting and polishing and tea making, but that's about all.'

Adam Turner came back into the shop. 'I'm sorry Ruth. I'm not going to be able to manage the shopping trip. I've got to go and look at some stuff in a house in Sheffield. The owners can only meet me today.'

'It's OK,' Ruth said. 'No problem. I don't mind, Daddy, honestly.'

Adam Turner looked at Samantha. 'We were going shopping in town: to buy a party dress.'

'I'm going to Leeds,' Samantha said. She glanced at Ruth. 'How about coming along? You'll have more choice and you won't have your father smothering you.'

'No, I don't mind. I wasn't really bothered about a dress I'd only wear once.'

'It's your last day at the school,' Adam

Turner said. 'I'd really like you to have the dress.'

'If you like I'd help you choose,' Samantha coaxed. 'We could have lunch together. I'd enjoy it.'

'OK,' Ruth said half-heartedly. Then, realizing she must sound rude, injected more feeling into her voice as she added, 'It's very kind of you. I'd really appreciate it.'

As they walked beneath the archway and down the passage through the buildings, Samantha wondered why a seventeen-year-old should be so uninterested in an outfit for an end-of-term party. They turned into the rear yard and Samantha began to pick her way across the cobbles to the car.

'Gosh, is this yours?'

'Do you like it?' Samantha unlocked the doors of the Ferrari.

It's . . .' Ruth shrugged and let out a little laugh, '. . . wickedly fast looking.'

They slid on to soft leather. Samantha keyed the ignition and the car's exhaust reverberated throatily as they returned beneath the archway, merged with the traffic on the Leeds-Bradford road, and headed for the motorway.

Samantha sensed the girl was looking her over and risked a sideways glance.

Ruth met her gaze. 'Are you daddy's girlfriend?'

Samantha laughed at the bluntness of the

question. 'Do I look old enough?'

'Nobody seems to bother about age anymore. Anything goes.'

'Don't worry. I'm not your father's girlfriend. I'm just trying to find some interesting pieces for the public rooms of a hotel, that's all. And I have to go to Leeds, and clothes-shopping is a major indulgence of mine. We'll get you something really stunning; something that'll make all those stupid boys sit up and take notice.'

Ruth laughed. 'They do seem rather silly, but I don't particularly want to be noticed. I certainly don't want anything provocative.'

Samantha risked another glance. The girl was sitting very primly, the hem of her grey skirt tugged well below her knees, her hands modestly folded on her lap.

They circled the roundabout that linked feeder roads to the motorway. The Saturday morning traffic was light; the stretch of motorway beneath them deserted. Samantha accelerated hard down the slip road, shifting through the gears.

Ruth let out a scream that rose in pitch and intensity as they roared on to the motorway and crossed to the outer lane. In a few stomach-lurching seconds they were doing a hundred and forty miles an hour. Samantha took her foot off the accelerator and allowed the car to coast down to a sedate seventy.

Ruth was laughing, her hands on her

flushed cheeks. 'Gosh, that was thrilling; like the big dipper at Blackpool, only more so. Do you do that often?'

Samantha laughed. 'Hardly ever. Only when I feel the need to let myself go.'

'What a car! It's wicked!'

Samantha hoped she'd broken through the girl's reserve. It wasn't shyness. She was intelligent and seemed mature for her years: very calm and composed. The flow of relaxed talk had started. Samantha decided all she had to do now was keep the conversation going and wait for an opportunity to find out what was troubling her.

*　　　*　　　*

Ruth seemed unable to muster any enthusiasm for the shopping expedition. Between breakfast at Harvey Nichols and a late lunch at Bibi's, she purchased a black dress and a sequined black jacket. Covering her arms and shoulders and getting the hem below her knees seemed more important to her than cut and style.

The shoes she chose after lunch were low-heeled and plain. Ruth had fixed ideas about what to wear. Samantha soon realized that if she wanted the girl to be relaxed with her, she had to keep her thoughts about clothes to herself.

On their way back to the car, Samantha

posted a package to Gavin Rudd, also known as James Noble, the London gigolo. She was returning the diary she'd taken from his jacket pocket, and didn't care to have a Barfield postmark impressed across the stamps.

They motored home slowly, cool in the air-conditioned interior of the car. After they'd cleared the city centre, Samantha glanced at Ruth and said, 'Why did you ask me if I was your father's girlfriend?'

'Mummy and daddy have split up. I just thought he might have found someone else. And you are very glamorous.'

Samantha laughed softly. 'You think your father's girlfriend would have to be someone glamorous?'

'Mummy was. She still is when she gets dressed up. Anyway, that's what seems to appeal to men, isn't it?'

'Did it upset you very badly, their splitting up?'

'I suppose so,' Ruth said slowly, as if she wasn't completely sure. 'Mummy's always been busy with her job and daddy's been away a lot, trying to get his new business going, so it wasn't the wrench it might have been. And I was working for exams. I had to concentrate hard on that and I suppose it took my mind off it all. They're still friendly.'

'How did the exams go?'

'OK, I think.' She sounded uninterested rather than confident.

'What about university?' Samantha asked.

'I've not done anything about that. I suppose I've sort of let it slide. And anyway . . .' She looked down at her hands.

'Anyway?' Samantha prompted.

'I may decide not to go.'

They swept on in the coolness of the car, the only sound the muffled drone of an engine that was little more than idling.

Samantha hadn't got anywhere and they were almost half way back to Barfield. She could understand Adam Turner's concern now. There was something, she was sure of it. She had to be more direct. She didn't have the luxury of endless time.

'Do you want to tell me about it?' she asked softly.

'Tell you about what?'

'Tell me what's eating you up inside. What's made everything so grey and dismal for you?'

Ruth let out a bitter little laugh. 'I didn't realize it was so obvious. And dismal's the perfect word for it. Dear God, I've never felt so awful.' She fumbled for her handkerchief and began to weep silently.

Samantha pulled the car into a lay-by and switched off the ignition. She found a box of tissues in the glove compartment and offered Ruth a handful as she said, 'Have you talked to your mother about it?'

Ruth shuddered. 'I couldn't. It's so awful. I've never felt so embarrassed and ashamed.'

'How about your father, or one of your teachers. They're nuns, aren't they?'

'I think daddy ought to know, but I wouldn't know how to begin to tell him. And the nuns wouldn't understand. Really, I couldn't! Talking to Sister Annunciata or Sister Winifred about this would be too embarrassing for words.'

Ruth's head sagged forward and the weeping erupted into sobs. Samantha unfastened their seat belts, put her arms around her and drew her close. She retrieved the tissues, began to dab Ruth's eyes and wipe the mucus from her nose. 'Would you like to tell me about it,' Samantha asked softly. 'I've seen just about everything. I couldn't be shocked.'

Ruth dragged in a deep breath. 'It was just before Easter, just after daddy had gone to live at the shop. Mummy said she was going to some professional function, so I went to stay over at Jenny's: she's a school friend. Whenever there was no one in the house, I used to go and stay there. I go to daddy now.'

Ruth took the fresh tissues Samantha handed her, dabbed at her eyes and nose and tried to get the sobbing under control. After a while she went on, 'When it got late I realized I'd not brought my night things. Jenny's house is quite close to mine, so we all got into her father's car and he drove us over. They stayed outside while I let myself into the house to get my overnight bag. I'd packed it but I'd left it in the hall.'

'When I got in I knew there was something strange. Mummy's shoes had been kicked off in the hall and her dress and tights and other things were just scattered up the stairs. I was stupid,' she moaned. 'Stupid, stupid, stupid. I should have realized, but I didn't.'

Samantha understood now, but she had to be sure, and the telling would be cathartic. 'Realized what?' she asked.

'What was happening,' Ruth moaned. 'I should have grabbed my bag and just walked out, but she was supposed to be in Manchester and . . .' She dragged in another breath, let it out in sobs as she went on, 'You can see into mummy's bedroom when you turn round the landing. Heavens, I could smell it when I was at the top of the stairs: perfume and sweat and stale aftershave. The door was wide open. At first I thought she was being raped, and then I heard her, moaning out this awful filth and him holding her by the thighs while he did it.'

'Him?'

'A man: a muscular young man with close-cropped blond hair. He didn't look any older than the boys some of the girls at school go out with. They didn't have anything on. She was sprawling on pillows piled up on the bed, he was standing between her legs, and it was so violent.'

Samantha took the last of the tissues and

passed them to her. 'Violent?'

'The way he was doing it to her. It was so animal. And it was my mother. *My mother!* Moaning out that lewd filth and him grunting, and there was this slap, slap, slap, as his stomach kept hitting the back of her thighs.'

'Dear Lord! Oh my dear Lord.' A fresh wave of sobbing racked her body.

When Ruth spoke again her voice was little more than a whisper. 'I thought it would be so gentle and tender. Not like that. And it was my mother, with that man, saying all those vile things, telling him to . . .'

Samantha slid her arms around her again, gave her shoulders a squeeze. It's over,' she said. 'You accidentally saw something you were never meant to see. Something very private: a glimpse into your mother's secret life.'

'But it was so unspeakable. I thought she was being raped until I heard what she was saying.'

'Lovemaking's so intensely private, Samantha said. 'Men and women lose themselves in it. You're not really conscious of what you're saying or doing.'

Ruth went on sobbing into the soggy tissue, head bowed.

'Like I said,' Samantha murmured huskily, 'By sheer chance you saw something secret. It wasn't your mother's fault. She'd every reason to think they were alone in the house.'

'What should I do?'

'Nothing. Just try and forget it. Put it right out of your mind and get on with your life.'

'But what about daddy?'

'What about daddy?'

'Shouldn't I tell him?'

'If he doesn't already know, finding out would crucify him. If he does, discovering that you know would only make it worse because it's something he wouldn't want anyone to know, especially his daughter.' Samantha gave her shoulders a squeeze. 'Just try and forget it. And when you make love you'll do it in a way that pleases you.'

Ruth turned, red-eyed and blotchy-cheeked. 'I don't think I will,' she said. 'In fact, I'm sure I won't.'

Samantha raised an eyebrow.

'I'm going to be a nun.'

'Did you decide that after you'd seen . . .' She let the question hang in the air.

Ruth shook her head. 'I've been thinking about it for more than a year. I'd made my mind up long before that. I don't know how I'm going to tell daddy. He won't understand. Mummy won't either. I've been trying to pluck up courage to tell them, but I was finding it so hard to cope with what I'd seen that night I just couldn't face all the argument. They'll be so disappointed in me. They're not into religion.'

'I suppose the nuns at school know?'

'Well, yes. But they don't know everything.

They think I'm going to join their teaching order, but I'm not. I want to go into the Carmelite convent at Kirk Edge.'

'An enclosed order? Be a contemplative?'

Ruth brightened. 'You know about religious orders?'

'Just the odd fact I've picked up along the way.'

'I suppose you think I'm stupid?'

'Why should I think you're stupid?' Samantha demanded.

She shrugged. 'Your car, your clothes. You look so elegant and glamorous, so worldly.'

'I don't think you're stupid,' Samantha said softly. 'I think it's a beautiful thing that you want to do, and you mustn't let anyone stop you.'

Samantha looked at her in silence for a while, then asked, 'Why the Carmelites? Why shut yourself off from the world?'

'Last year they took some of the sixth-formers to Kirk Edge to see a nun being professed. Before that I'd only thought about the teaching order, but after going to Kirk Edge I knew that I really wanted to enter Carmel. It's very complicated. I don't really understand it myself. It's just something I know I've got to do.'

She was looking down at her hands, folding and unfolding a piece of tissue. Presently she said, 'I don't know how I'm going to tell mummy and daddy. They'll go ballistic.'

'Would you like me to tell your father?'

'Isn't it something I should do myself?'

'Occasionally it's best to take the easy way out; save your energy for bigger fights. And you've had a lot to cope with this year: big decisions, exams, discovering your mother's secrets. Why not let me break the news?'

'I suppose it would be a load off my mind.'

'Are you going back to the shop?' Samantha asked.

'Daddy was going to drop me off at home.'

'Why don't I take you home, then go on to the shop and tell him while we're sorting out the furniture for the hotel?'

'Would you? It would be such a relief.'

They were driving through suburbs to the north of Barfield now. Samantha turned into a tree-lined crescent and pulled up outside a dignified-looking detached house with a big gable that projected over bay windows. A red front door had carriage lamps on either side of it and the whole place looked tidy and well maintained.

'Thanks,' Ruth said, 'For the day and everything.'

'That's OK. I enjoyed it.' Samantha reached behind the seats, pulled out the dress shop bags, and handed them to Ruth. 'Forget what you saw,' she said. 'Try and think of it as an unpleasant dream. And never tell your father. Even if you think he knows, never reveal to him or your mother that you do.' She reached over and took her hand. 'Promise me?'

Ruth nodded.

'And don't let anyone stop you going into that convent.' She gave Ruth's fingers a squeeze. 'Do you hear me?'

The girl laughed, ran her arms around Samantha in a brief embrace, then climbed out of the car with her bags.

Samantha watched her walking up the drive in her green-striped red school blazer, her grey skirt and drab stockings. She seemed more erect and there was a new lightness in her step.

Samantha let out the clutch, left rubber on the tarmac, as she accelerated hard around the crescent, heading back to the main Barfield road.

*   *   *

The shop door had been wedged open to let in the cooler, early evening air. Samantha went through to the workshop and found Adam Turner in his carpenter's apron, trimming the edges of some blue leather he'd just applied to the top of a tiny gilded desk.

He glanced up. 'You're back. Where's Ruth?'

'She said you'd agreed to drop her off at her mother's, so I left her there.'

'Of course.' He nodded, remembering.

Samantha sat on the low carpet-covered worktable and removed her sunglasses.

'Did you find out anything?' Adam Turner

eyed her expectantly. He was trying to rub glue from his fingers with a rag.

'What little there is to know. She's made a decision about her future and she's been worried about how you and your wife will react to it. She couldn't face telling you.'

'Decision?' He stopped rubbing his fingers.

'She's decided to become a nun.'

His eyes widened and his big features slackened, making him look a little comical. 'Be a nun,' he snorted. 'But that's ridiculous. She's not even religious.'

Samantha tried hard not to smile. 'You may not know as much about your daughter as you think, Mr Turner.'

He slumped down on to a trestle, his shocked eyes staring blankly across at Samantha. He seemed suddenly to remember something, and blurted out, 'But what about the violent sex business? What did she mean when she was asking me about that?'

Samantha shrugged. 'Probably something she'd seen on late-night television. There's no romance any more and the sex is coarse and explicit. If I was seventeen and thinking about becoming a nun, I'd be disturbed by the things they show on television.'

'But she doesn't have to join the order. She can teach without doing that. She doesn't have to become a nun.'

'It's not quite like that, Mr Turner.'

'I don't know what you mean,' he

demanded.

'She wants to enter an enclosed order; be a contemplative.'

'Enclosed?'

'The Carmelites. They have a convent at Kirk Edge, on the moors above Sheffield.'

He seemed stunned. He looked down at his hands, picking absently at the remains of the glue on his fingers. After a few moments he glanced up and said, 'What do you make of it?'

Samantha eyed him steadily, thought fleetingly of her own life, of her guilt and fears, of the terror and hatred etched on to the faces of men she'd killed, of her sometimes precarious state of mind. 'I think it's wonderful,' she said huskily. 'A bright light in a dark, shitty world.'

'But she's so beautiful, so clever. It's an unbelievable waste of a life.'

'We have to think very hard about our own lives before we say things like that,' Samantha retorted bitterly.

She watched him looking her up and down, at her flimsy shoes, the low-cut summer dress that fitted a little too well, at glossy red lips and carefully made up eyes.

'Don't *you* think she's mad, Miss Quest?'

Samantha tried to hold back a smile. He obviously saw her as the very antithesis of the holy nun, more whore than Madonna, a woman of the world who'd give him a straight answer.

'I don't think she's mad at all, Mr Turner,' she said softly. 'And I think you should support her and help her as much as you can.'

He drew in a deep breath and tried to pull himself together. 'This has been quite a shock. I was expecting some trouble with a boy or maybe a man.' He shook his head. 'I must pay you. I'll get my cheque book.'

Samantha rose to her feet and reached for her bag. 'It's OK, Mr Turner. I enjoyed the day. Have this one on the house.'

'But I must.'

'Forget it.' Samantha slid her sunglasses on.

'Pick something from the shop then,' he insisted. 'If I don't seem grateful it's only because I'm so shocked. Pick anything you want, except this desk. Someone's fallen in love with it. She came to the shop to look at it again today and I've promised it to her.'

Samantha laughed. 'The kind of life I lead, the last thing I want is some antique to dust and polish. But you're very kind.'

She half turned to leave, then looked back and said, 'If you really want to do something for me, just be gentle and supportive for Ruth. And when she shows you the dress, tell her how nice she looks.'

He grinned ruefully. 'It's not haute couture then?'

'Dior wouldn't use it for a duster.'

She could hear him chuckling as she stepped out into the balmy summer evening.

CHAPTER SEVEN

Emma Taylor stared nervously at the borough architect across the paper-heaped desk. Under the neatly trimmed moustache, his lips had an unhealthy purplish tinge, and his eyes were bleak. He'd abandoned his style-statement bow tie and pink shirt. Today his neckwear was dark blue and conventional, his shirt white.

'Someone phoned you?' Emma repeated.

Stanley Jackson nodded. 'He said I'd regret it if I brought people on site to check the reinforced concrete work. He said I had to leave well alone. I said *I'd* decide what work was satisfactory and what wasn't. He got nasty then, said I should forget the pension because I'd never live to draw it.'

Emma gazed at him, shocked into silence.

'Did you mention reinforcement to what's-his-name, the job QS, before you suspended him over that rock business?' Jackson asked.

'Darren? Yes. I told him I was going to talk to you about having all the concrete work checked. I wanted him to know I was serious about it all.'

'So he could have passed that on to Bartlets?'

Emma nodded. 'But surely Bartlets wouldn't make threats. It's unthinkable. Could you recognize the voice?'

'No. And he was careful; made the call from a public phone. I still can't believe it. I've never encountered anything like this in thirty years. It scared my wife. I wasn't having that, so I phoned the police.'

Stanley Jackson swung his chair until he was gazing towards a window that was being peppered by heavy summer rain. He stroked his neat little goatee beard, then looked back at Emma. 'Couldn't get the chief constable. They said he was at some meeting to discuss the terrorist threat and they'd no idea when he'd be available. They got me the most senior man they could find on the Crime Squad. He refused to come to my home and he wouldn't let me go in and see him; blighter even avoided giving me his name. He wasn't helpful. In fact, he was rather dismissive. Just said they couldn't act on an anonymous phone call. Told me to get back to them if I had any more trouble. It's too dammed late when you've had the trouble.'

Emma gave him a disbelieving look. 'I can't think anyone at Bartlets would make death threats. It's preposterous.'

'Someone's making threats,' Stanley Jackson said bleakly.

'What about the engineers?' Emma reminded him. 'You were going to arrange for them to check all the reinforced concrete work.'

'You might well ask,' he snorted. 'The two

engineers who were due to go on site yesterday both reported sick. What do you make of that?'

They eyed one another in silence. Rain had stopped beating against the windows and watery sunlight was gleaming on wet roofs.

Jackson sighed. 'At least one good thing's come out of that dreadful bombing business. They've arrested Quadir, the councillor who was giving me all the trouble at the committee meetings. And the chief executive was telling me they've taken in Al-Banna's son: Al-Banna's the chairman of the Development Committee.'

'I suppose we'd better leave it alone for the time being?'

'We've got to, Emma. You've done everything you could. You discovered it, suspended what's-his-name . . . ?'

'Darren,' Emma prompted.

'That's right, Darren. You informed me; arranged for Internal Audit to do a check with one of your people. How's that going by the way?'

'They started yesterday. It'll take the best part of a week. But it's only a formality. The rock's been massively over-measured. I think we may have to claw back another twenty-thousand in the next interim.'

Stanley Jackson frowned. 'The man who phoned about the reinforcement didn't mention the rock. They seem to be separate issues. It's as if Bartlets are uptight about the rock and someone else is worrying about the concrete. Don't rush the re-measure, Emma. Let them take their time. In fact, it might be a good idea if you told your senior QS, Mallins, Martin . . .'

'Markham,' Emma corrected.

'That's it, Markham, to be meticulous, take all the time he needs to make sure we can't be challenged on the figures. That should give us time to see how all this develops.'

Emma rose and began to head for the door.

'We'll keep this to ourselves, Emma?' Stanley Jackson's scared eyes flickered over her face.

'Of course.'

'And Emma?'

'Yes, Mr Jackson?

'I think we should exchange confidential reports on it all. You note what you've discovered and set out the cost implications. I'll make a detailed record of the phone calls and the meetings I've had with the committee. You know, just in case.'

*   *   *

Emma got behind her desk. She felt sorry for Stanley Jackson, worried for them both, and more than a little relieved that the responsibility was all his. She'd passed the problem on and he had to deal with it. But what had he meant when he'd said, "Just in case"? Just in case of what?

She glanced down at her organizer and suddenly realized she was lunching with Hugh Dixon today. The initial rush of irritation faded. He'd be a welcome distraction from all this trouble, just as he'd been a distraction when she'd been threatened with redundancy after Christmas. On a sudden impulse, she picked up the phone and keyed in one of the general office numbers.

'Is that you, Alex?'

She caught the mumbled affirmative.

'I've got to go to Leeds this afternoon. We're briefing lawyers about the arbitration on the Staveley Street School contract. I might be back and I might not. If I'm not, would you get Mr Markham to sign the mail?'

*   *   *

Hugh Dixon's face lit up when she walked around the corner of the bar. He rose to his feet. 'Emma! Thank God. I thought you weren't coming.'

He helped her into a chair. 'Can I get you a drink?'

'Brandy,' she said. 'With ice and a splash of American dry.'

'There's just the usual pub stuff on the menu. Nothing special. Is there anything you fancy?'

'A sandwich would be fine,' Emma said. 'Chicken. And perhaps we could have coffee?'

He went over to the bar, ordered the food and brought back the drinks.

'You're looking great,' he said, then sipped at his glass of wine.

'You're not looking so bad yourself,' Emma said, laughing.

His face suddenly became serious. 'I've missed you, Emma. I can't begin to tell you how much I've missed you.'

'That's ridiculous,' she protested. 'We only spent an evening together.' She didn't care for his intensity. It scared her a little.

'I can't forget it. I can't get it out of my mind.' He reached over and took her hand, began to caress the palm gently with his thumb.

His fingers are warm and dry, Emma thought, not clammy like Adam's. 'Try not to be so serious,' she said softly. 'We just had a pleasant time together, and . . .'

'Who's beef, who's chicken?' A waitress had appeared beside the table holding two plates.

Emma pulled her hand from Hugh's and said, 'Chicken.' The waitress allocated the plates. 'Would you like the coffee now?'

'In about ten minutes,' Hugh said. Then, turning back to Emma, asked, 'And what?'

When the waitress had gone, she said, 'And I'm older than you. A good deal older.' She looked down at the sandwiches and had a pleasant surprise when she saw the delicate triangles of soft bread ringed by fresh salad.

'I don't care,' he said. 'Anyway, you don't look it.'

'You're very sweet. And I'm flattered. But you're just infatuated. When the newness has worn off you'll see me as I really am.'

He swallowed a mouthful of sandwich, then reached over and took her hand again, squeezed it hard as he said, 'I can't express myself very well when I'm talking about things like this, but I'm not stupid. I do see you just the way you are, and you're gorgeous when you're naked.'

'Shh!' Emma blushed. She glanced around. The adjoining tables were empty and they were sitting some distance from the crush around the bar.

'You're all I think about,' he insisted. 'I can hardly sleep. I've been going mad trying to get through to you on the phone. I nearly called your home.'

'Don't ever do that,' Emma said sternly. 'That's another thing you've got to remember: I'm married.' She'd no intention of revealing that Adam had walked out. A husband at home was a useful way of controlling the situation.

'I'd marry you,' he said. 'Divorce him and I'll marry you tomorrow.'

'You're crazy,' Emma protested. 'You don't know a thing about me. We've only spent an evening together.'

'I'm trying to tell you how I feel, Emma.'

She looked across at the long, handsome, distressingly boyish face with the serious eyes and the mouth that was eminently kissable. It was utterly unlike Adam's fleshy features and slack lips. And Hugh was young in mind as well as body. Everything was simple to him, so easy, so live-for-the-moment.

'I suppose I'm trying to say I love you, Emma,' he said softly.

She reached for her drink and said, 'Try not to be so serious, Hugh. It was pleasant the other evening. It was more than pleasant. But that's all it was.' She could feel her cheeks burning.

'I've not been able to bear it.'

'Bear what?'

'The way you've been avoiding me. I know you have. I suppose I embarrass you and you're hoping I'll just go away.'

'That's not true,' Emma protested, realizing he wasn't so immature that he hadn't realized exactly how she felt. 'You don't know how busy I've been. And things are very difficult for me at the moment. And I'm married, for God's sake. I've been married for almost twenty years. It colours the way I think about things. It's not that simple for me.'

'You're telling me I make you feel guilty?'

'No. I mean, well, yes, I suppose you do.' She didn't feel the slightest bit guilty, but letting him think she did would help him to accept that she couldn't abandon herself to a full-blown affair. 'I'm married, Hugh,' she repeated gently.

'Do you sleep together?'

His question shocked her. 'I'm sure that's my business.'

'It's just that I can't bear to think of another man making love to you,' he said simply.

Emma gazed at him for a few moments, then said, 'He's my husband, Hugh.'

'Then you do?'

'You and I,' Emma said hastily, 'we've just been snatching a few hours of pleasure together. You knew I was married. You're not being reasonable about this. You've got to lighten up or I'm going to walk away. You're so intense you're scaring me.'

'I'm sorry. I can't help it.' He was squeezing her hand hard.

Half a dozen office workers came down to their end of the room, pushed a couple of tables together and sat quite close, chattering noisily.

Emma tugged her hand free.

'It's difficult to talk now,' Hugh said irritably. 'How about coming back to my flat. It overlooks the river.'

'Take me home,' she said. 'The car's being serviced and I walked here.'

'Will your . . . ?'

'My husband's working. He won't be home

103

until around six,' she lied, putting a time limit on the assignation. Ruth would be coming in then, but she didn't want to tell him she had a daughter.

They left their food mostly untouched, their drinks half-finished, and headed out to his car. He held her hand but they hardly spoke during the short journey to her house in Auckland Crescent. As they pulled on to the drive, she noticed a white van parked outside the house opposite. Having some more work done, she mused. There surely couldn't be much else they could do to the place.

'Bring your briefcase,' she said, as they were emerging from the car. 'If any of the neighbours are watching they might think you've come to do some business.'

Hugh did as she asked and stood behind her while she unlocked the red front door. When they stepped inside the hall he leant back against the door, heard it slam shut and the latch click home. He reached out.

Emma felt his hands on her hips, his thumbs stroking the small of her back. She leant against him, felt him kissing her neck while his hands slowly caressed her thighs.

She found it impossible to understand. She couldn't explain it. When he kissed her, when his hands began to move gently over her body, she melted. It was lust; overwhelming sexual desire. She liked this man, found him pleasant, but she didn't feel any tenderness towards him.

It was just the way his caresses made her body sing.

'Let's go into the breakfast room,' she said breathlessly. 'It's on the side of the house. The neighbours won't see me drawing the curtains in there.'

His hands rose slowly over the swell of her stomach and began to fondle her breasts. 'Not the bedroom?'

'No. The breakfast room.' She pulled herself free, kicked off her shoes, then grabbed his hand and led him through a door a little way down the hall.

'Switch the electric fire on,' she said, then crossed over to the window and drew the curtains to shut out the brightness of the summer afternoon.

Emma returned to him, grasped the lapels of his jacket, and pulled him on to his knees beside her on the thick Chinese rug.

The electric fire was radiating its orange glow over them now.

She struggled with the knot in his tie, then tugged it free. He slid his arms around her, almost lifted her as he began to kiss her on the mouth.

She drew away. 'Don't make my lips puffy. And don't mark me. Whatever you do, don't mark me where it can be seen.'

He slipped off his jacket. Emma began to unbutton his shirt, then, made impatient by desire, just tore it open and peeled it down over his back.

The youthful body was hot and hard, tanned and fragrant. She rubbed her cheek against his chest and clung to him; abandoned herself to the anarchy of the senses.

*　　　*　　　*

Jack Slater watched the silver Ford Granada turn on to the driveway of number sixty-five. He'd been lucky. He'd not had to wait long. The woman climbed out first; dark-haired, shapely, quite a looker: then the man. He was wearing a dark suit and holding a briefcase. Jack Slater's eyes narrowed. Close-cropped blond hair, handsome in a pretty-boy kind of way: it was *him*, the jogger. When he'd driven past him last night he must have been on the home stretch.

He looked a bit younger than his wife. Betty was a lying bitch. He wasn't some scrawny, middle-aged bastard. What the hell had she been doing with him all that time in his poncey antique shop?

Jack gripped the steering wheel, trying to control his anger. His chest tightened when he felt like this, and his head throbbed with a dull ache. He unbuttoned his collar and dragged in some deep breaths. Continually getting into this state wasn't doing him any good.

The woman's skirt tightened over pert buttocks as she reached up and struggled with the key, then she pushed open the red front door and her husband followed her inside. Jack went on staring at the house after the door had slammed. An idea was scuttling, like a spider, along the grimy passageways of his mind. Betty wouldn't be spreading her legs for the baby-faced bastard much longer.

* * *

Adam Turner thumbed the bell. It felt strange to be back at the house, having to ring the bell instead of just stepping inside. He didn't notice Emma peering around a curtain in the bay window. He was pressing the bell again when the door opened.

'What's wrong?' Emma asked the question automatically. He looked more worried than he usually did, and she couldn't think of any reason why he should suddenly appear on the doorstep after four months.

'Nothing's wrong. I just need to talk to you. Can I come inside?'

She drew the lapels of her cream satin dressing gown together and opened the door wider. He stepped into the hall.

'Come on through. I'll make you a drink. The kettle's just boiled.'

As they went down the hall, he began to push at the breakfast room door.

'No,' she said hastily. 'Come through to the kitchen. I've been sorting papers out in there

107

and it's a bit of a mess.'

The kitchen was just as he remembered: gleaming white units, marble effect worktops, a polished hardwood floor. They'd had it done the year before he left, paid for it with a legacy from one of Emma's aunts.

She spooned coffee into a mug. 'Couldn't you have telephoned?'

'I've been trying to reach you at the office all afternoon. They said you'd gone to Leeds. I've been ringing you here for the past hour.'

Emma poured in hot water. She'd have been in the shower with Hugh. She wouldn't have heard a lightning strike, let alone the phone ringing. She added a dash of milk, then carried the mug over to the pine table where he was sitting.

'You're looking wonderful,' he said softly. Her cheeks had a rosy blush and her eyes were strangely luminous, yet sleepy. He watched as she unwound the towel from her hair and began to rub it dry.

She didn't respond; didn't even look at him. Nothing's changed, he thought bitterly. Whenever he'd said anything about the way she looked she'd ignore it or change the subject. Eventually he'd realized she saw compliments as sexual overtures; something she didn't want, something she had to nip in the bud in case they led to him doing more than talking.

Adam sipped his coffee and watched her

drying her hair. It was as if he'd never left, as if the past four months at the shop had been a dream.

Emma became uneasy in the silence. She felt like urging him to get on with it, to tell her what the problem was, but he looked so pathetic she couldn't be that abrupt.

'It didn't take you long,' she said lightly.

'I don't know what you mean.'

'To find yourself a girlfriend.'

Adam laughed. 'I've still no idea what you're talking about.'

'The glamorous piece with the expensive car who took Ruth to Leeds on Saturday.'

'That's Miss Quest. In a way, she's why I'm here, but she's not my girlfriend.'

'Ruth said she wasn't, but I'm not that stupid.'

Adam laughed, enjoying his wife's jealousy but suspecting it was probably feigned.

'You must know her well or you wouldn't have let her take Ruth to Leeds. The dress is bloody awful, by the way.'

'Ruth chose it, and there's a reason why it's so awful.'

'Are you sleeping with the Quest woman at the shop?' Emma was rubbing her hair briskly, tilting her head so that it fell away from her face.

'The only woman I want to sleep with at the shop or anywhere else is you,' he muttered. 'She's a private investigator. I hired her to find out what was wrong with Ruth. Ruth's been upset about something, and I was worried sick.'

'That sounds normal,' Emma said. 'I can't remember a time when you weren't worried or depressed about something.'

Ignoring the remark, Adam said, 'She found out that Ruth wants to be a nun. That's why I'm here. I think we need to talk about it.'

Emma let out a mocking little laugh. 'You wasted your money. I could have told you that for nothing.'

'You knew?'

'Sister Annunciata called me to the school last week and told me Ruth intends to enter the order.'

'Why didn't you tell me? Couldn't you have picked up the phone?'

'You walked out, Adam. If you'd been here we'd have gone together. I didn't have time to contact you.'

She was perched on a high stool. The satin dressing gown had parted, exposing plump thighs and calves. The flesh was milky-white, and, here and there, he could make out the faintest tracery of blue veins beneath the skin. He knew what the flesh of her thighs felt like. He could almost feel it now, the silky-smooth skin, warm and soft under his hand. He let his eyes linger on the parting of the robe where tiny black satin pants were curving around her stomach.

Adam felt a sudden, painful, rush of desire. And with it, anger at his frustration, anger at her power to arouse such intense feelings in him. But the humiliation was the worst. He knew she no longer wanted him to touch her: that she found him repulsive.

'Sister Annunciata doesn't know everything,' he said, truculently.

Emma stopped rubbing her hair and looked at him. 'What's that supposed to mean?'

'Ruth doesn't want to go into the teaching order. She wants to enter some Carmelite place near Sheffield. It's enclosed. They're locked in. It's like being in a prison. Christ, I wish we'd not tried so hard to get her into that dammed Catholic school.'

Emma met his gaze for a few seconds, then continued to rub her hair. Adam went on staring at her. Through the loose folds of cloth he was catching glimpses of her breasts. Apart from the black satin knickers, she was naked under the robe.

Suddenly feeling an overwhelming sense of loss, he dragged his eyes away and blinked back tears. Pictures were flickering on the screen of a small portable television on one of the worktops. The sound had been turned down, but he could see a bearded rabbi in front of that synagogue they'd bombed in London. He couldn't hear the words, but he was sure they'd be wise and profound. He needed some wise words, someone to tell him why women went cold and how to cope with the bitterness when they did.

'Well?' he asked.

'Well what?'

Emma was beginning to sound irritated. That's how it had been before he'd left. She'd talk to him for a while, and then she'd begin to sound irritable and dismissive.

'What do you think about Ruth going into this enclosed order?'

She stopped rubbing her hair. 'I've had a week to think about it, Adam. If it's something she really wants to do, then we've got to let her do it. And if we can't look pleased about it, at least we shouldn't look miserable. If she was taking drugs or sleeping around and getting pregnant, we'd have something to worry about.'

'You don't think we should try and reason with her; try and talk her out of it?'

'She's almost eighteen, Adam. If we try and talk her out of it we'll make her more determined. We've got to leave her alone.'

'Does she know that you know?'

'I don't think so.'

'It's such a waste of a life. I'd like to talk to her, and I think we should talk to her together.'

'What's the point,' Emma demanded. 'We don't particularly like it, but it's her life and we'll only upset her if we start going on and on about it.'

Adam tore his eyes away from Emma's breasts, pushed his almost untouched coffee towards the centre of the table and stood up. He began to move towards the door.

'You're going?'

'I don't think we've anything more to say to one another.'

'I'll show you out then,' Emma said, a little taken aback. She'd been toying with the idea of asking him to take a look at the shower door she and Hugh had sprained that afternoon.

He didn't speak; he didn't even answer when she said good-bye at the door. She watched him walk to the road, climb into his battered Citroen car, and drive off. He didn't look back.

Emma went into the breakfast room, opened the curtains, and switched off the electric fire. She folded her suit and draped it over the back of a chair, then picked up her tights and underwear and headed for the utility room.

Carpet burns on her shoulder blades and lower back, a bruise where she'd slipped against the shower door; the afternoon had been memorable. She closed her eyes. She could still feel the tiles, cold against her back, Hugh's big hands under her thighs, lifting her, holding her, while water that was almost too hot to bear pelted down on them.

It had never been like that with Adam.

113

Hugh was one of those men who knew what to do to a woman. And she'd abandoned herself to it; gone with the flow. It was raw, primitive, exciting. It wouldn't last. She wasn't stupid enough to think it would. He was younger than her in body, and much younger in mind.

Things would be easier when Ruth left for university or went into that wretched convent. With Adam and her daughter out of the way, she'd be free to indulge herself a little. When Hugh was drying her after the interlude in the shower, he'd asked her to go away on holiday with him. She'd not given him an answer, but the idea appealed. Maybe early next year they could escape the worst of the winter together.

The back door slammed.

'Mummy? You in?'

Emma heard Ruth's footsteps in the kitchen and went through. 'Your father's been.'

'Daddy? Ruth's face brightened. 'Is he still here?'

Emma shook her head. 'He came to tell me you'd decided to become a nun.'

The girl suddenly looked apprehensive. 'And how do you feel about it?'

'We're both very happy for you, if that's what you really want to do.'

'Oh, Mummy!' Relief shone from Ruth's face and she threw her arms around her mother. 'I'm so glad. I thought you'd both hate me for it.'

CHAPTER EIGHT

Jack Slater reversed his van on to the rutted track that marked the boundary between the school and open fields. He checked the dashboard clock, then switched off the engine and the lights. It was almost midnight. The blond jogger, the poncey owner of the antique shop, the bastard who was screwing his wife, should be passing soon. He'd sort him, and then he'd sort Betty, the fat slag. She was no better than the other wives at the rugby club, no better than his mother.

Everything was sliding out of control. It was like being a kid again, suffering that endless succession of uncles, with their beer and tobacco-tainted breath and big hands and oily hair. Money for the cinema when his dad was on the late shift, something for the amusement arcades or to spend around town when he was on days. His big, placid, trusting, ever-loving dad: pit, pigeons, pints and a packet of Players. His dad never suspected and he never told him, even when he was older and understood. It would have destroyed his dad, or his dad might have killed his mother. And in spite of everything, he loved her like a good son should.

His head throbbed all the time now, and the pains in his chest were beginning to frighten him. When he'd sorted the jogging bastard who was screwing Betty, when the block contract was finished, he'd go and see the doctor. Meanwhile, he'd have to try and keep the rages under control.

Staying calm wasn't easy. He couldn't think straight any more. Whenever he closed his eyes, tried to snatch a little sleep, all he could see were those black-polythene-wrapped bundles of decaying flesh. And no matter how often he washed his hands and changed his clothes, he could still breathe in that cloying, putrid smell. Jack shuddered and wound the window down to let in a little of the cool night air. Thinking about the bitches had made his chest hurt.

What about Betty? He couldn't make his mind up about her. He ought to kill the bitch, but perhaps he should just kick the shit out of her, put her in hospital, then sell the house and find some quiet little place in Spain. He'd thought about going to the shop and catching them at it; smashing the place up, killing the bloke, then killing her. But Frank had the street surveillance camera locked on the place. He'd have been videoed, caught in the act. He had to stay calm, get the bastard as he jogged home along this unlit stretch of road.

Jack checked the time. It was twelve-thirty. He'd wait until one, then call it a night, get back to the factory, fill the cavity he'd left in the block and leave everything tidy for the men when they came in later that morning.

*   *   *

Fire alarms were clanging, deafening and insistent. Borough architect, Stanley Jackson, was running down gloomy corridors where thick smoke blotted out the light and clung to him, slowed his movements. He had to find a fire escape or a window; any opening that would get him out of that dingy place.

He was becoming frantic. The members of the Development Committee were all around him now, upbraiding him, goading him with scathing voices.

'What possessed you, Jackson, to design a building without windows or doors?'

'And no fire escapes.'

'A dereliction of duty.'

'Only an imbecile would create such a fire risk.'

'You'll be dismissed.'

'With immediate effect.'

Urdu, Bengali, Romanian, Albanian, Arabic: a polyglot chorus that, with the limpid simplicity of dreams, he could understand.

Stanley heard the roar and crackle of flames, the rumble of falling masonry. The voices began to scream at him. 'You designed it, you get us out.'

'I'm burning.'

'We're all burning.'

'Find a way out, Jackson, and do it quick.'

Oily black smoke, viscous and choking, slowed his movements to a crawl. Alarm bells were clanging, clanging, echoing down endless corridors . . .

Stanley jerked up, gasping for breath, his face sheened with sweat. Downstairs, the phone was ringing in the hall. Beside him, her hair in curlers, Peggy was sleeping peacefully.

It could be his daughter, Tracey! Jackson swung his legs out of the bed, groped for his slippers, then loped across the landing and stumbled down the stairs. His student daughter was a constant worry. Any call in the night would probably be from her.

He lifted the receiver.

'Jackson?' It was a male voice he didn't recognize. It held the faint remnants of an accent he couldn't place.

'Speaking.'

'You've let me down, Jackson. I don't like that, I really don't.'

'Who is this?'

'You've been to the police. When I told you to stay off that building site I told you to keep your mouth shut.'

'How do you know I went . . .'

'I know when you cough,' the man interrupted. 'And I don't like you blabbing about concrete and reinforcement. Poking your nose into things is bad enough; running to the police really upset me. And it won't get

118

you anywhere. The boys in blue know you're just a pompous old fool.'

'I'm the borough architect,' Jackson puffed. I've a duty to check work on site.'

'You're a pathetic little jack-in-office. Don't give me that garbage about duty,' the voice sneered.

Stanley Jackson bristled. *Pathetic little jack* . . . How dare he? 'I don't think you understand,' he snapped back. 'As the architect responsible for the project, I decide what's acceptable or what's not acceptable,' then his voice rose to a shout as anger gripped him, 'and I'll inspect whatever I damn well please.'

He crashed the phone down, stepped into the sitting room and switched on a table lamp. A cut glass decanter and the tumbler he'd used earlier that night glittered in the light. He poured a generous measure and tried to get his breathing under control as he sipped at the amber spirit. Fear was intensifying his anger now, and his heart was pounding.

The phone began to ring again, shrill and insistent. It might wake Peggy. He didn't want her upset by all this. He put down his glass, returned to the hall and picked up the phone.

'Don't do that to me again, Jackson,' the voice snarled.

'I'll do what I bloody well . . .'

'Your daughter, Jackson: I know all about her, too.'

'My daughter? What about my daughter?'

'Second year student at Leeds University. Has a bedsit on Thornlea Road. Pretty face, nice ripe body.'

'I don't know what you mean,' Jackson gasped.

'What I mean is, if you don't keep off that site and your mouth shut, we'll take her.'

'Take her?' Jackson's voice was little more than a whisper.

'Pick her up, take her out of the country, put her to work in the business.'

'Business?'

'Are you completely stupid, Jackson? Whores, prostitutes. She'll take a little breaking in, but when she's in a strange country, without papers, where she can't speak the language, she'll soon realize what's good for her. We're experts at making women do as they're told.'

'You wouldn't dare.'

There was some relaxed laughter, then the voice said, 'Don't count on it, Jackson.'

The earpiece clicked and a faint buzzing came down the line.

Stanley Jackson swallowed hard. He stood in the silence of the hall for a few seconds, suddenly icily calm. He knew now what he had to do. He cradled the phone then headed up the stairs to wake his wife.

*   *   *

120

Betty Slater rummaged in the tiny velvet lined box on her dressing table, trying to find more hairpins. Jack hadn't come home. He'd worked all night again. She couldn't predict his mood when he did that. Sometimes he was too tired to be unpleasant: other times he was filled with that cold anger that tipped him into violence. Best thing was to get out of the house before he came in. She abandoned her search for pins, took a length of blue ribbon from a drawer and tied her hair up with that.

Seeing that policewoman had helped her a lot. She didn't have to put up with Jack's moods. She certainly didn't have to put up with him hitting her. And the pain in her side was easing now and she could move more easily, thank God.

Betty stared at her reflection. She hadn't used make-up for months. It was an act of defiance: challenging Jack. And she had a deeper reason for taking so much trouble with her appearance, something intuitive, a reason she would never have admitted to herself.

The sticking front door rattled open, then crashed shut.

Sweet Jesus! He was back before she'd got out. Betty scooped her things into her bag, slid her feet into her shoes and headed down the stairs.

Jack was leaning against the front door, thumbing through that morning's mail without bothering to open the envelopes. He looked grey and ill. He seemed suddenly older. That coarse animal vitality was deserting him.

Betty rounded the bottom of the stairs and managed to get halfway to the kitchen door before he glanced up.

'Where you going?'

'Out.'

'You're not going out dressed like that. Not without me, you're not.'

'It's only a summer dress.'

'You look like a fucking tart. Get the dress off and wipe that stuff off your face before I wipe it off for you.'

'It's a respectable Marks and Spencer's dress, Jack. It's a nice morning and I'm going into town.' She was trying to sound reasonable.

Jack tossed the letters on to the floor. 'You're not going out looking like that. Come here.' He lurched towards her.

Betty ran into the kitchen, took her mobile phone from her bag, keyed it on then began to blurt out, 'I went to the police yesterday; Domestic Violence Unit. The number's keyed into the phone. I just have to press a button and I'm straight through. The policewoman wanted me to make a formal complaint, but I didn't. They sent me to the hospital. They've x-rayed my side; it's in the hospital records now. That's why the policewoman made me go.' The torrent of words held him transfixed in the doorway. She was holding the phone with outstretched arms, pointing it at him as if it could emit some lethal ray.

'Bitch!' He snarled. 'You fat stupid bitch. Going to the police could give me big trouble right now.' He moved into the room, a towering presence.

Betty dodged behind the table, bag in one hand, phone in the other. 'Don't, Jack. Don't you dare lay a finger on me or I'll press this button and call the police.'

Cold blue eyes glared at her out of a face that was grey with tiredness. His jowls were dark with a two-day growth of stubble and sweat glistened on his brow and nose. And then his anger suddenly left him. He hadn't the energy to sustain it. Working around the clock for days had exhausted him. He dragged a chair from beneath the table and dropped down on to it.

Betty glared at him across the tiny room. She felt no pity, only relief that he was too tired to hit her.

'You're going to see that baby-faced bastard at the antique shop, aren't you?'

'I might,' she said. 'I'm going to buy that desk, Jack. When he's finished restoring it, I'm going to have it.'

'And he's having you, isn't he?' Jack snarled.

'Don't be stupid. I'm only interested in the desk.'

'Don't call me stupid,' he yelled. 'And the bugger must be desperate; *young* bloke like that fancying a fat old cow like you.' He glared at her, dragged in a few noisy breaths, then said menacingly, 'You've been to see him every day for the past week. Been in there almost an hour some days. He's been poking you, hasn't he?'

Betty looked down at him, trying to make some sense of the cold lights glittering in his eyes, the ugly contortions of his handsome face. Jack must be crazy. The owner of the antique shop had big uneven features. No one would call him baby-faced. No one would call him young.

Presently she said, 'You're sick, Jack. You need help.' She went on staring at him in silence for a while longer, then added softly, 'I used to love you; really love you. Now I hate you. I didn't think I could ever hate anyone as much as I hate you.'

He sagged back in the spindly chair, leering up at her sleepily. 'You're just like all the rest, Betty: a dirty slag. A fat dirty slag. When I'm ready, I'll make you pay. And that poncey young bastard won't have his hand in your knickers much longer. You wait and see.'

'No one's got his hands anywhere, Jack. All I want is the little gilded desk.'

She reached behind her, groping for the back door handle, all the time keeping her eyes locked on his. She grasped it, got the door open, and backed out. When she lost eye contact, she turned and ran down the side of the house, across the unfenced front lawn and out into the road.

The antique shop was closer to the town, but only a short walk away. She'd go and take another look at the desk; see if it was finished. She glanced nervously over her shoulder before turning the corner at the newsagent's. Then, skirt swaying, high heels tapping on the pavement, she strode out into the sunlit summer morning.

＊　　＊　　＊

Adam Turner lit the old gas ring and lowered the kettle on to the flames. He was nursing a hangover and needed tea badly. Seeing Emma almost naked the previous evening had intensified his dreadful feeling of loss, and left him sexually frustrated. And their vaguely unpleasant conversation had made him irritable and depressed. It had taken half a bottle of whisky to blur the edges of his despair, to make him sufficiently comatose to find sleep in the canopied bed in the flat above the shop.

Needing more than tea to ease the dull ache, he climbed the stone stairs that rose up the side of the workshop and entered the flat. He stepped behind an elegant green and gold Japanese screen that was, until it was sold, hiding a kitchen sink, some cupboards and a microwave oven. Searching through a drawer, he found a blister pack of tablets, swallowed two with a mouthful of water, then made his way back to the workshop.

She was there, bending over the desk, examining the gold tooling around the blue leather. She hadn't heard him coming down the stairs, so he paused and studied her.

Her coppery-blonde hair had been gathered up and tied with a blue ribbon that was a near perfect match for the summer dress she was wearing. Its sleeves were short and her pleasantly plump arms were lightly tanned. High-heeled blue-and-white shoes were showing off shapely legs and ankles, and the styling of the dress revealed some very womanly curves.

When he stepped down on to the concrete floor of the workshop, she looked round.

'Hope you don't mind,' she said. 'I thought you wouldn't be far away, so I came in to take another look at my desk.'

She was calling it 'my desk' now, Adam mused. Out loud, he said, 'It's OK. Help yourself.'

She'd turned towards him. The scoop neck of the dress was rather low. He tried hard to keep his eyes on her face and off the dramatic cleavage between her breasts. She'd made-up her eyes and put on lipstick. She'd always looked attractive when she'd called before, but Adam thought she looked quite beautiful now.

She blushed and seemed embarrassed.

'I'm sorry,' Adam said. 'For staring, I mean.

It's just that you remind me of someone.'

The lid of the kettle was rattling and water was boiling on to the gas ring. He crossed over to it. 'Would you like some tea? I'm just making myself a cup.'

'That would be nice.'

He dropped tea bags into mugs and poured on the hot water. 'Milk and sugar?'

'Just a little milk. Who is it I remind you of?'

Adam laughed, a little embarrassed himself now. 'It's a woman in a picture, not a living person.'

'Have you got the picture in the shop?'

'Heavens, no. Wouldn't be here if I'd owned it. I'd have sold it and been living in luxury.' He carried the mugs over. 'Earl Grey. That OK? It's all I've got, I'm afraid.'

Betty took the mug, said, 'Thanks,' then pulled a face when she tasted the tea. She sat down, next to the desk, on the low carpet-covered work bench.

'Who was she, then?' She took another sip and didn't pull a face this time.

'Who was who?' Adam was captivated by this voluptuously sexy woman and his thoughts were wandering.

'The woman in the picture.'

'Oh, her.' He laughed. 'Miss O' Murphy. She was a French King's mistress. Can't remember which one: Louis something or other. François Boucher painted it.'

'And I remind you of her?' Betty sipped the

127

tea. It was a bit perfumey but it grew on you.

'When you first came into the shop I thought I'd seen you somewhere before. Seeing you with your hair gathered up like that made me realize you remind me of the woman in Boucher's picture.'

'Is it in Leeds art gallery?'

Adam shook his head. 'It's in the Wallraf-Richartz Museum in Cologne. On an upper floor.' He watched her taking delicate little sips at the tea, then allowed his gaze to wander over the voluptuous form that was shaping the blue dress so emphatically. He lifted his eyes back to her face and said, 'I saw it when we were on holiday in Germany a few years ago. I thought it was one of the most erotic images I'd ever seen.'

Erotic! Betty wanted to ask him what he meant but thought better of it. Instead, she asked, 'You said "we"; you're married, then?'

Adam's smile became a frown. 'I am, but I'm not living with my wife. I left last Christmas. I've got a make-do flat above the shop.'

'Was it someone else?'

He let out a bitter little laugh. 'Nothing like that. She's just obsessed with work. It's all she thinks about. I got sick of being ignored.' That wasn't strictly true, but he wasn't going to reveal to a near stranger that he couldn't stand the lack of physical affection, the absence of tenderness, any more.

'My husband's the same,' she said, 'but it's

made him ill.'

'I'm sorry,' Adam murmured, at a loss for something more meaningful to say.

'I mean really ill,' Betty went on. 'Mentally. He's become violent. I had to go to the police this week. I talked to a woman in the Domestic Violence Unit.'

Adam gazed across at her. Her body had stiffened and her chin was quivering. 'I really am sorry,' he repeated, with more feeling. 'I can't imagine how a man could hit a woman, no matter what she'd done.'

'And I haven't done anything,' she said tearfully. 'He's just insanely jealous. It's making him crazy.'

Big brown eyes, moist with unspent tears, swept up and held his. Adam knew then that if he said the right words he'd sooner or later end up in bed with her. He met her gaze for a while, and then she put her cup down and looked at the desk.

'Is it finished?'

The opportunity was lost. He knew he'd regret not having spoken words that would have signalled an interest in her. Would-be seducers had to seize the moment.

'Almost,' he said. 'There's just a bit more gold leaf to go on one of the legs.' He crossed over and turned the desk so they could see the red patches where the original gold leaf had worn through. He was standing above her now, looking down at her hair and some white lace under the bodice of her dress. She was wearing a flowery perfume and the warmth of her body was sending up a cloud of fragrance. He was already regretting the lost opportunity.

'Will it take long?' She looked up at him.

'Another couple of days. I've had to break off to deal with other things.'

'Other things?'

He nodded towards some sheets of thick, rough plywood. 'I've got to make shutters for the windows and doors. The trouble's spreading and if they break into the shop I could lose everything.'

'Trouble?'

'Some lunatics firebombed houses near the old railway works last night and the Hindus and Muslims started rioting. It was on the breakfast news.'

'I heard the police sirens going and the helicopters buzzing around, but I didn't realize what it was,' Betty said. She'd spent the night, clutching her mobile phone, waiting for the sound of Jack's van door slamming. Her terrors were domestic, not out on the street. 'It's been awful in Leeds and Bradford, but I didn't think we'd have trouble here.'

'Let's hope it stays on the other side of town,' Adam muttered.

'Seems selfish of me, but I've hardly given those bombings in London and all the rioting a thought. I've been a bit taken up with my problems with Jack: Jack's my husband.' Betty stood up and reached for her bag. 'I'd better let you get on.' She brushed past him, soft and fragrant. 'I'll see you tomorrow. We'll have to talk about delivery: that could be difficult.'

She disappeared into the shop, then suddenly popped her head back through the opening and said, 'By the way, thanks for the tea. It was very nice.'

CHAPTER NINE

'Samantha?'

'Speaking.'

'It's Marcus. I've been trying to reach you for twenty-four hours.'

Samantha said nothing, just sat there, watching the images flickering on the television screen while she listened to the hiss on the line. She'd been expecting and dreading the call.

'You there, Sam?' He demanded.

Encryption was leaching the character out of his voice, making it sound metallic, but she could discern his agitation. She'd never heard him anything but calm and unruffled before. He wasn't laughing down the line and calling her Peaches now. He wanted something; he wanted it badly.

'I'm here and listening,' she said huskily. 'And I was here through the night. If you'd wanted to reach me . . .'

'I was at the Ministry until dawn,' he interrupted tetchily. 'The Anti-Terrorist Squad caught a couple of blokes with a flask of ricin on the approach road to a waterworks in north London. It's been bedlam here.'

'You managed to keep that out of the news,' she said wryly.

'Are you kidding? Things are becoming unstable enough without starting a water poisoning panic. Did you get the profiles?'

Samantha reached across the sofa and picked up a sheaf of papers. 'I was just going to feed them through the shredder.'

'I trust you're satisfied?'

She glanced at the photographs of the corpses; at the bands of colour in the DNA profiles. The photographs were enough. The men were Halabi and Mosharif, she'd no doubt about that. 'I am as far as these two are concerned,' she said. 'But what about Nasari, the American national? He's the one who kept getting close to me.'

'I think I've got round that problem for you.' His voice had taken on its customary urbane tone now he was talking about something he had under control. 'The Russians are prepared to sign him over on the pretext that you're going to escort him to Berlin for transfer to the CIA. You'd kill him when he tries to escape. The Russians daren't let him go back to the States; he knows too much about their war in Chechnya. And they understand your need to be sure he's dead: that the best way of achieving that is for you to do the execution yourself. The Russians are still grateful to you, Sam. I'd no difficulty with them, just our own people.'

'The Americans would know it was a set up,' Samantha said.

'They'd be pretty sure but they could never be certain. And upsetting the Americans is the least of our worries at the moment. The last surviving member of the Berlin group would be dead, there'd be no one left who could identify you, threat lifted, and you're back in business.'

Fleeting gaps in the metallic speech when the encryption failed made his words even more chilling. It was all so simple to him. And 'back in business' was the last thing she wanted to hear. Marcus hadn't made the arrangements as a favour to her. He was working through his own agenda.

Samantha closed her eyes and listened to the hissing on the scrambled line. She could still see the tangled wreckage of the bus, smell the pungent odour of burning oil and plastic. The blast had torn off most of her sister's clothes and the flames had burnt her hair away. Her niece was barely recognizable; her brother-in-law's body was never found.

'Sam . . . Sam, you still there?'

'I'm here,' Samantha murmured huskily. 'It

133

sounds OK to me. When do I fly out?'

'Next week sometime. We'll get you out to Moscow and the Russians will arrange transport from there. I'll finalize the arrangements and get back to you.'

Despite herself, she felt a weight lifting. 'Thanks, Marcus, I'm grateful. I really do want this business over with.'

'We want you back, Samantha.'

'I don't know whether I can come back.'

'I've got to ask you. The situation's dire.'

'I'm burnt out. I don't know if I can face it again.'

'Queen and country, Samantha.'

Pompous prat, Samantha thought. 'You've already tried Queen and country, Marcus. I don't give a damn about your relatives. And it's the politicians who've got the country into this mess. Give the minister a gun and tell *him* to shoot the terrorists.'

'Republican cynic,' Marcus retorted, without humour. 'What about the tube bombings? What about the synagogue? Isn't that where your sister and her family were going when they were killed in Berlin? You'd be protecting the lives of ordinary decent people, Sam. Avenging *all* the innocents they've murdered. Surely you can identify with that?'

'You're out of order, Marcus. My sister and her family are my personal business.'

'The hate gave you an edge, Sam; made you

134

the best we had.'

'I can't go on hating and avenging.'

'Chaos is at the gates. These crazy fundamentalists are going to take us back to the dark ages if we let them. And you wouldn't be fettered. You'd have a free hand.'

She didn't speak, just sat there, watching a pair of irrepressibly cheerful early-morning news presenters pretend to flirt with one another. After a long silence she said, 'We can't stop them, Marcus. If some fanatic wants to shove Semtex up his arse and ride on the tube, or pour ricin in a reservoir, there's nothing anyone can do about it.'

'We can take them out before they go for a ride on the tube. We can hold back the tide.'

'Haven't I done my share of holding back the bloody tide?' She was suddenly close to tears. Her body was shaking. She'd thought she was stronger, that the two years she'd spent in this quiet backwater town had begun to heal her, but this conversation with Marcus was revealing how fragile her mental state was.

'Sam . . . Sam? You OK?'

'I'm fine, Marcus, absolutely fine.' She hoped the encrypted line would conceal the shake in her voice.

'Maybe we should talk about this after the Russian trip. When that's out of the way . . .' He was going to say *You might feel better about it,* but some instinct told him the words would probably alienate her even more.

'You'll contact me about the flight arrangements?' she asked.

'Of course. And I'll keep you posted generally. The PM might declare a state of emergency before the end of the week. If he does we'll move in and start doing what we should have been doing years ago. I'll call you tonight if there are any developments: tomorrow if not. OK?'

Samantha switched off the phone. Reaching for the bottle at the side of the sofa, she poured a couple of measures into her tea and began to sip the mixture.

They were desperate. Marcus wouldn't have been authorized to make the arrangements with the Russians if they weren't. They wanted their killer back; their deft, silent, efficient eliminator of the enemies of the state. But why did it have to be her? Why the hell should she go on killing for the incompetent bastards?

The whisky began to ease her distress and the trembling subsided. When she next lifted the cup to her lips it no longer rattled against her teeth.

*   *   *

Emma Turner leafed through the quantities for the Chase Lane Comprehensive extension, looking for obvious anomalies. She wasn't too happy with the preliminary clauses. When the wretched Ethnic Minorities Welfare Centre

136

job was running smoothly, she'd re-write the standard text herself.

The phone began to ring. She lifted the handset.

'It's Jackson here, Emma.' The voice was breathy and nervous. 'I'm at Leeds-Bradford airport. Peggy and Tracey are with me. In ten minutes we'll be on a flight out.'

'Out?'

'Yes, out. Out of that bloody hell-hole. I had another call: in the middle of the night. Whoever it was knew I'd contacted the police about the threats. He said he'd harm Tracey if I made any more trouble. Said it was a waste of time complaining to the police because they're in his pocket. The place is rotten to the core, Emma. I'm not having my wife and daughter exposed to that sort of thing.'

'What do you want me to do?' Emma asked lamely.

'I suggest you do nothing. Keep away from that site and carry on working as normal. I'm just putting you on your guard and warning you not to bother going to the police. You have a daughter, don't you?'

'Yes, Ruth,' Emma whispered.

'Well, the threats they were making to me about my daughter were unspeakable, so watch yourself.'

'Who's going to take over?'

'The project architects will have to sign the certificates in my name. That's the arrangement I made when they refused to replace my deputy, what was his name?'

'Vincent; Vincent Branwell,' Emma prompted.

'That's it, old Vincent. Forget this call, Emma. I don't know how to deal with the situation, so I'm clearing out for a while. Just be careful . . . Oh!' He suddenly remembered something. 'Those notes I made on the committee meetings and the threatening phone calls are in an old blue folder at the back of the filing cabinet in my office: the bottom drawer. It's not locked. You ought to get them, put them with your notes and hide them somewhere.'

'Does your secretary know you're not coming in?'

'No. I've only phoned you because you're involved and I had to warn you. Don't say anything to anyone. Just get the papers from my office when Monica's on her lunch break. Got to go, Emma. They're calling our flight. I'll be in touch.'

Emma put down the phone. She'd no idea who was involved in the conspiracy, so she couldn't discuss it with anyone. It was a mess and she was on her own. She couldn't even confide in Adam. He'd stalked off in a foul mood after his visit yesterday and he wouldn't be disposed to help. And her juvenile lover was just that: juvenile. He was fabulous in bed but utterly useless for anything else.

She picked up the phone and keyed in a general office number. After too long a wait she heard a voice mumbling a name.

'Is that you, Jeremy?'

'That's right, Mrs Turner.'

'Try to sound a little brighter when you answer the phone, Jeremy. It's usually our first contact with the public.'

'Sorry, Mrs Turner.'

'Is Mr Markham there?'

'He's out doing the rock re-measure on the Ethnic Minorities Welfare Centre.'

'He left me a copy of the bills for the school extension. Would you tell him it's all OK and to go ahead and put the job out to tender.'

'Will do, Mrs Turner.'

Emma replaced the receiver. Trainees: they were hopeless these days. You had to tell them how to dress, how to answer the phone. And the reminder that Markham was doing a painstaking re-measure of the rock only increased her unease.

When she leant back in her chair she could still feel the soreness of the carpet burns on her back. She craved the distraction Hugh Dixon provided. Whenever she was under pressure, sex helped her cope with it. But she needed help not distraction, and it had to come from outside the system. Suddenly remembering the private investigator Adam had hired to find out what was bothering Ruth, she lifted the phone and dialed the shop.

'Barfield Fine Arts and Antiques.'

'Adam, that investigator you hired: was she any good?'

'Impressive,' Adam said. 'Highly recommended by Jack Walters. She did a job for a friend of his. She's expensive but quick, so she's probably not that expensive in the end. Why are you asking?'

'A colleague,' Emma said. 'Business problems. He needs someone capable and discreet.'

'I'm sure she'd be that.'

'How much did she charge you for checking Ruth out?'

'Didn't charge. Said she'd enjoyed the day.'

'Ruth told me she bought her breakfast at Harvey Nicks and lunch at Bibi's,' Emma said.

Adam laughed. 'That must have set her back a few quid. When she said she didn't want paying I asked her to pick something from the shop, but she refused. I don't think she's into antiques.'

'You've not lost it then?'

'Lost what?'

'The Turner charm; getting her to do the job for free.'

He let out a bitter little laugh. 'It doesn't seem to work on you any more.'

Emma ignored the remark. She didn't want that kind of conversation with him. 'Do you have her phone number?'

'Hold on a sec.'

The phone clattered down and she caught the faint sounds of papers being moved, then a scraping as he slid the handset across the desk. 'Here it is. It's for her mobile; I don't have her office number. Got a piece of paper?'

She said she had and recorded the numbers as he read them out.

'Thanks,' she said. Then, feeling a little awkward and realizing she couldn't just ring off, asked, 'How are you?'

'Fine. Same as yesterday. Absolutely bloody fine,' he said bitterly, then crashed the phone down.

Moody beggar, Emma muttered, then dismissed him from her mind and pressed the studs on the phone to clear the line. She was half-way through dialing the number Adam had given her when she thought better of it. She'd use her mobile or, better still, find a public phone and make the call from there.

*　　*　　*

A mid-week wedding party was being held in the upper rooms of the hotel. Samantha watched guests enter, promenade across the foyer, then climb the main stairs. It seemed to be a lavish affair: half-a-dozen bridesmaids, page boys, the bride in a fussily extravagant white dress and carrying the train over her arm.

Emma Turner was late. She'd sounded

141

agitated on the phone, but it was the family connection that had intrigued Samantha and persuaded her to agree to the meeting.

The sound of happy chatter was floating down the stairs now. The wedding party was moving into a higher gear. Guests were still arriving: men in morning suits, women in their wedding best; small hats, big hats, hats with flowers and hats with feathers. Samantha took pleasure from the spectacle, the current of life, the celebration of a happy event. It was helping her to push Marcus's request for her return to the back of her mind. And her pleasure was without envy. Matrimony was something she did not seek for herself.

Samantha recognized a few of Barfield's great and good: the deputy chief constable, the new and salaried mayor, some businessmen and their wives. Since she'd come to live in the town she'd read the local papers and the glossy county magazines, and her memory for names and faces was photographic. She had perfect recall. It was one of the gifts that had made her so useful to the organization.

'Thanks for the steak dinner, Jane.'

Samantha turned and glanced up at the man in the morning suit standing behind her. The almost too handsome face was smiling down at her.

'Why, Mr Noble! Or are we Mr Rudd today?'

He laughed, stepped in front of her and sat

142

in the chair facing hers. 'Noble,' he said. 'I'm with a barrister. She's in chambers in London. We're wedding guests.'

'I had noticed,' Samantha said, looking him over. 'You look pretty nifty in that morning suit.'

He laughed. 'And you're devastating in that green silk dress. It matches your eyes. Is it Chinese or Japanese?'

'A French evocation. It came from a little boutique behind Harrods.' She allowed her gaze to wander over him again, then said, 'No hard feelings?'

He smiled. 'Of course not. I wasn't kidding when I said I adore women. And you're probably the most glamorous woman I've ever met.'

'Don't you ever stop working?' Samantha asked.

His expression became serious. 'Honestly, I really do mean it.' He eyed her across the low table for a moment, then asked, 'Would you have shot me?'

'Mmm, I might,' Samantha said. 'But not to kill. And I wouldn't have damaged your business equipment.' She smiled at him in a teasing way, then asked, 'Did I manage to scare you?'

He looked thoughtful. 'I knew I'd be OK if I did what you wanted. But it was your eyes more than the gun; they're so compelling; they blaze out at you. I've never seen eyes like

143

yours before.'

He picked up his grey top hat and gloves from the table. 'I'd better go. I noticed you when we came in and I slipped away to say hello when Sonya went to talk to some old school chums.'

'Talking about old chums,' Samantha said, 'you ought to be careful here. You've bedded the wives of most of the members of the local rugger team.'

'Rugger team?' he repeated nervously.

'Barfield Barbarians. And they deserve the name. They're seriously big and very violent.'

'God, you really are scaring me now.'

'They've seen your photographs. They were very impressed.'

He glanced around nervously. 'Are any of them here?'

'I didn't notice any faces amongst the guests, but I missed you, so I could just as easily have missed them. You'd better be careful.'

'Thanks for the warning.' He rose to his feet, very elegant in the morning suit. Then he frowned and said, 'I hope you don't mind my asking, but are you one of Sappho's sisters?'

Samantha threw back her head and laughed. 'You're very sweet,' she said, still laughing. 'And no, Mr Noble, I'm neither a poet nor a lesbian.'

He had the shame to blush. 'Forgive me. I can't seem to help putting my foot in it with

144

you. It's the eyes. They're mesmerizing. One can't think.'

He sauntered away over thick carpet. When he reached the foyer he glanced back, smiled and waved, then headed up the stairs to his client.

As he did so, a woman in a black business suit left her chair on the far side of the room and came towards her.

'Miss Quest?'

'That's right, and you're Mrs Turner.'

The woman nodded, then sat in the chair vacated by James Noble. 'I saw you were with a friend, so I waited until he'd gone.'

'Not a friend,' Samantha said. 'Just an acquaintance.'

'He's unbelievably handsome. Is he an actor?'

'In a way,' Samantha laughed. 'His face has certainly been his fortune. Shall we have a drink?'

'I'd like that,' Emma Turner said. 'Can I get them?'

Samantha caught the eye of a boy in a uniform and crooked her finger. He came over.

She looked at Emma. 'Gin and tonic?'

'That would be fine.'

Crimson lips parted as she gave the boy a dazzling smile. 'Gin and tonics; not too much ice, plenty of lemon, and make them doubles.'

The boy blushed, mumbled something

145

inaudible, then loped off to the bar.

Samantha turned and studied the woman. She could understand Adam Turner still finding her attractive. With a seventeen-year-old daughter, she was probably at least forty, but she didn't look her age, and a lot of men found the fuller figure sexy. Her dark-brown hair was drawn back and tied with a black ribbon. She was probably trying to look professional rather than overtly feminine.

'I was expecting someone a little older,' Emma Turner said.

Samantha smiled, watched the woman's worried brown eyes flicker over her nervously. She didn't speak.

Presently Emma blushed and went on, 'My husband gave me your telephone number. I hoped you might be able to help me.'

'How could I do that?' Samantha asked.

Emma stared down at the old leather briefcase lying on her knees. 'It's rather worrying,' she said. 'In fact it's frightening.' She glanced back at Samantha and studied her face with anxious eyes.

'Just tell me about it,' Samantha said. 'Then I'll see what I can do.'

'Gin and tonics, madam.' The boy in uniform had re-appeared with a tray. Cotton-gloved hands reached out and laid paper napkins on the table, then he set down tumblers and two bottles of tonic water.

Samantha gave him another brilliant smile.

Still blushing furiously, he seemed captivated by the embroidered dragons that writhed over the bodice of her dress. She dropped a note and a couple of coins on to the tray. 'Keep the change,' she said huskily.

Emma viewed the spectacle with a wry amusement. When the boy had wandered off, she emptied the tonic into her glass and said, 'Thanks. You'll never know how much I needed this.'

'So,' Samantha said. 'Tell me all about it.'

Glossy red lips, heavy eye make-up, and a Susie Wong dress hadn't disconcerted Emma. She felt she could trust Samantha. She went over the events of the past week and handed over the notes she and Stanley Jackson had made. After recounting her last telephone conversation with Jackson, she sat back in her chair and watched Samantha leaf through the papers. Relaxed yet alert, Emma thought. Just like a cat.

Samantha glanced up. 'You say Jackson doesn't think this business with the rock is connected with the threats about inspecting the concrete?'

Emma nodded. 'He thought Bartlets were whingeing about the rock, but someone else is worried about the concrete being checked.'

'Threats are uncommon, I suppose?' Samantha asked.

'Absolutely unprecedented. The contract has arbitration provisions. If contractors feel

147

aggrieved they don't hesitate to use them. Claims take up far too much time. And Bartlets are reputable. I can't imagine anyone less likely to make threats.'

'And you're sure they've missed the reinforcement from the foundations?'

Pursing her lips, Emma thought about that for a moment. 'It was certainly missing from the stretch I saw in the trench. If it had been there the bars would have protruded from the last concrete pour.'

'What if it's not there?' Samantha asked.

Emma shrugged. 'They could underpin with the correct foundations. Or we could leave things as they are but make them insure against foundation failure. We'd deduct the cost of the reinforcement, of course.'

'Either way it would be costly to the contractors?'

'Very,' Emma said.

'But it's not something they'd threaten the borough architect about?'

Emma laughed. 'Absolutely not. It's rare, but things like this do happen. The contractors have to swallow the extra cost and carry on.'

Samantha leafed through the photocopied sheets. 'You said something about some huge concrete blocks, but they're not mentioned here. Where do they fit in?'

'They form a retaining wall across the top of the site. We've got to provide a road to a new housing development higher up the hill and the blocks hold back the fill under it. It's more usual to erect shuttering and pour the concrete on site, but the architects and engineers decided they wanted it doing this way. The finish on the pre-cast blocks is better.'

'These blocks; they're really big?' Samantha asked.

'About three metres long by a little more than two high and one deep. They come on a low loader, one block every working day, and they're craned into position. They fast cure them at the factory and the back filling can start straight away.'

'Cure?'

'Get the concrete up to its working strength. They use chemicals and steam to raise the temperature and get a quick set.'

'Bartlets make these blocks off-site, then?'

Emma shook her head. 'Not Bartlets. Specialist sub-contractors make them.'

'And where would they be?'

'There's only one firm in Barfield,' Emma said. 'I think it's called Slater's Pre-Cast.' She groped in the battered brief case for her mobile and took it out. 'I'll give the office a ring and ask the job architect to confirm that.'

'Don't,' Samantha said. 'Don't do anything that would let someone know you're checking things out.'

Emma paused, finger on button, and looked across at Samantha.

'You're pretty sure it's Slater's?' Samantha

149

asked.

'Almost certain.'

'Where's the factory?'

'On the Belmont Road Industrial Estate. It's down by the canal.'

Samantha gathered up the photocopied sheets and handed them back.

Emma's face fell. 'You can't help me?'

'I can look into it,' Samantha said. 'I might even be able to sort it out.'

'Won't you need these?' Emma held up the papers.

'Shred them,' Samantha urged. 'And put the originals in a safe deposit box or shred them, too. Having documents like that around could put you in danger.'

'But what about the borough architect: he wanted a record kept?'

'Forget the borough architect. He's scarpered. You've got to look after yourself.'

'What would your charges be?' Emma asked.

Samantha went through her patter about weekly and hourly rates and watched the colour draining from Emma's face.

'It's rather expensive,' Emma said bleakly.

Samantha smiled, reached over and covered the woman's hand with hers. 'Let's not worry about charges at this stage,' she said. 'I've got a feeling that someone else is going to fund this one.'

Emma nodded, still uncertain. She slid the papers and her phone into the case and pressed the catch down.

'This Slater,' Samantha asked thoughtfully, 'It wouldn't be Jack Slater, would it? Around forty, plenty of curly black hair, tall, handsome, a member of the local rugby football club?'

Emma shrugged. 'Sorry, I only know the firm's called Slater's Pre-Cast Concrete. We deal directly with Bartlets, the main contractors.'

Their eyes met. Emma felt a sudden twinge of envy for the younger woman's poise and clothes and beauty. It wasn't surprising she seemed to know so many handsome men. She smiled inwardly. If Adam thought he'd got half a chance with this exotic creature, he'd better think again.

Emma stood up. 'I'll have to get back. Can I leave it with you?'

'Why not,' Samantha said, and smiled. 'If there are any developments at your end, contact me on the number your husband gave you. I'll ring you at your home.'

Emma managed a bleak little smile, then turned and headed for the entrance. As Samantha watched her crossing the foyer, she noticed James Noble at the reception desk with a tall red-head. When they turned, the red-head was holding the keys to a room, an anticipatory smile on her attractive features. It looked as if James was going to have to earn his fee.

151

CHAPTER TEN

Samantha turned off the inner ring road and began to drive between new-looking industrial buildings surrounded by lawns and artfully placed islands of shrubs and small trees. Deeper into the estate, landscaping gave way to high steel fences enclosing the stack yards and lorry compounds of small factories fronting on to narrower service roads.

She was moving quite slowly now, trying to read sign boards that listed the businesses. When she'd almost reached the far boundary of the estate she saw 'Slater Pre-Cast Concrete' emblazoned along the corrugated sheeting of a structure that was bigger than the others and stood in a yard that took up the entire frontage of the last spur road.

Cruising on for another hundred yards, she found herself in a loading area that served a wharf on the canal. She climbed out of the air-conditioned Ferrari into the balmy warmth of a perfect summer evening. Three teenage youths were trying to propel a ramshackle raft along the murky water of the canal, and their splashing had fractured the reflected sunset into a million scintillating lights.

When they saw her they began to whistle, invited her to join them on the raft, regaled her with details of the sexual delights a trip down the canal would offer. She was mildly surprised. The oldest youth was no more than sixteen and she was wearing black jeans, black army boots and a black sweater: clothing chosen to hide her in the darkness, not increase her allure. She smiled to herself. Vikings lived on in South Yorkshire.

Ignoring them, she gazed across a compound stacked with concrete posts and beams towards Slater's factory. Three metal silos, rising above roof level, were ranged down one side. She surmised they were for cement and gravel. There were no windows in the metal walls, but a dozen roof lights were spaced out along the corrugated sheeting and a couple had been raised to let out the summer heat.

The gates to the compound were open and a white van was parked outside the factory doors. Sounds of machinery, humming behind metal walls, weren't loud enough to drown the evening song of birds in the bushes along the canal bank, or the drone of traffic from the now distant ring road.

Samantha climbed back into the air-conditioned coolness of the car, positioned it so she could see the factory entrance, then switched off the ignition. Sighing, she settled back into the leather. They worked late at Slater's Pre-Cast. All she could do was wait for darkness.

She must have dozed. The faint cheep-

cheep of her mobile phone roused her.

'Sam? That you, Sam?'

'I'm here, Marcus. Why are you calling me on this number?'

'Because I've been trying to get you on the encrypted line for the past six hours.'

'Sorry, Marcus. I've been out and about. You'll have to be careful.'

'I've had problems,' he went on. 'The deal I mentioned hasn't come through. The Americans are insisting that their share ownership be taken into account and the company bosses in London won't authorize your trip to clinch the take-over.'

Samantha pushed herself up in the seat. Marcus hadn't been able to talk his masters into the trip to Russia. 'I can't say I'm surprised,' she said.

'I'm still working on it,' he reassured her hastily. 'You must have seen the news on television tonight. Things are deteriorating. We're not managing to contain the situation. Another few weeks and no one will care who or what we take over.'

She didn't speak, just sat there, watching the factory while she waited for him to continue.

'I need you back in the team,' he said presently.

'You know the arrangement, Marcus. When the deal goes through and I've clinched the take-over I can start thinking about rejoining the company.'

'Bugger the arrangement. I'm desperate. If you won't do it for the good of the company, do it for me.'

Samantha let out a husky little laugh. 'You really are saying the wrong things now, Marcus.'

'Surely you could use the salary?'

'I do OK,' Samantha said, taking in the view from the car. It was almost dark now. Beyond the canal, powerful lamps were casting pools of light along some railway sidings, and there was a glow beneath the roof lights on Slater's factory.

'You can't be making much at that private investigation business.'

'You know about that?'

'You're getting quite a reputation, but you can't be doing very well in that grubby little town.'

'It's not a grubby little town. And there's plenty of business. The people lie and cheat, swindle and fornicate, pretty much as people do everywhere. The only difference is they don't keep banging on about being related to royalty.'

'You're a cynical bitch, Sam. Your old boss, Dearlove, used to say you were hard as diamonds, cold as ice, and he was right. You're the coldest little cock-teaser I've ever come across, and I've certainly met a few; they seem to gravitate to this place.'

Samantha began to laugh softly. The

situation was really stressing Marcus out. His patrician calm was cracking.

'This isn't funny, Sam. Not from where I'm sitting. Chaos has broken through the gates and it's screaming down the city streets.'

'Save the rhetoric for the minister's speeches, Marcus. You know what the deal was.'

'I've got to come up to Yorkshire the day after tomorrow,' he said, trying to lighten his voice as he changed tack. 'The minister's going to do walkabouts in Leeds and Bradford, make soothing noises about the riot damage. I'm going along to brief him and take a look at security out in the sticks. Could we meet and talk?'

'Don't see why not.' She could think of a dozen reasons why not, but she couldn't afford to antagonize him too much. Her long-term peace of mind demanded that the trip to Russia be authorized, and only Marcus could fix that for her.

'How about having dinner with me on Friday?'

'That could be pleasant.'

'I'm booked into the Commodore. They tell me the food's pretty good there. We could dine in my room. It'd be easier to talk. Should we say seven for seven thirty?'

'Seven sounds fine. And Marcus . . .'

'I'm listening.'

'It's just dinner and business talk. The

evening begins and ends with that.'

As she switched off the phone a vertical strip of light appeared between the huge sliding doors of the factory. It gleamed across at her for a few seconds, then vanished. She watched a tall figure, silhouetted against the white side of the van, climb into the cab. Faintly, across the stacks of concrete beams, came the whine of a starter, and the van rolled out and accelerated down the road. The man hadn't bothered to close the gates to the yard. Perhaps men were still working in the huge metal shed, or perhaps he didn't intend to be away for long.

Samantha swung her legs out of the car, sprinted the hundred yards to the gates and passed through. She crossed the parking area and checked the huge sliding doors. They were locked. She pressed her ear to the metal sheeting. Nothing disturbed the silence within.

She ran around the corner, to the side where the silos rose high above the roof. Climbing rungs were welded to the steel casings, but the lowest was located about ten feet above the ground. A crane on caterpillar tracks was parked just beyond the third silo. The roof of its cab rose above the bottom rung. She went over, grabbed a handle alongside the cab door and pulled herself up on to the tracks.

Moving round to the front, she clambered over a collection of hydraulic pipes and valves until she reached the roof of the cab, then climbed up the side of the silo. When she stepped on to a narrow platform alongside some loading doors, she found herself a few feet above the factory roof.

Beneath her, a lattice of girders linked silo to building. She clambered over a guardrail that ran around the platform, lowered herself on to the topmost girder, then stepped down on to the corrugated sheeting. The roof pitch was shallow. Climbing up to the open roof light wasn't difficult.

Samantha poked her head inside and peered down. Light was escaping from the door of an office built inside the cavernous space. It relieved the gloom sufficiently for her to make out some huge concrete blocks on what looked like a production line. She groped in the pocket of her jeans for a coin and tossed it down towards the office. It pinged on the concrete floor then rattled against some metal containers. She watched and waited. No one emerged from the office.

The top of the nearest block was no more than five feet below her. After making sure the stay holding up the roof light was secure, she swung over the cill and lowered herself until she could feel the block beneath her feet.

In the darkness she almost fell into a hole. Dropping to her knees, she shone a pencil torch down a narrow cylindrical shaft and saw it was around two metres deep. She shuffled across the top of the block, discovered a second shaft, then climbed down a wooden ladder to the factory floor.

When she moved the ladder and checked the top of the block nearest to the doors she found the shafts had been filled with concrete. Care had been taken to make the surface smooth and uniform, but slight differences in texture confirmed the presence of the holes.

Samantha made for the office. Drawings of the blocks were pinned to the walls. The network of reinforcing bars looked complicated, but there was nothing to indicate internal shafts.

The drawers of a battered old desk contained the usual office clutter, and a filing cabinet was crammed with folders marked with individual job numbers. She found the file for the Ethnic Minorities Welfare Centre and leafed through it: correspondence with Bartlets, copies of the quotation, a progress chart, copy invoices and a schedule of payments received. It all seemed tidy, well organized and normal.

She checked her watch. She'd been inside the place almost half an hour. She was pretty sure the man with the van was coming back and didn't want to linger much longer. Leaving the office, she made a quick tour of the factory floor. It was everything she'd imagined it would be. Drums of chemicals, steel reinforcing bars graded by size and held in racking, feed chutes from the external silos, a gantry crane, and a concrete mixer with a drum that reached up to the roof tie bars. Lit by what little light escaped from the office, the shadowy pipes and tanks and girders were like sinister things in a dream.

Samantha directed the torch beneath a bench that supported bar bending machinery, saw an untidy bundle of black plastic sacks. She tugged it out, kneaded it between her fingers and felt something. She identified the sack and shook the contents on to the floor. In the beam of the torch she could see a pair of women's worn shoes and a single shoe that was almost new, all high-heeled, all cheap. Wrapped inside a black nylon underskirt were two pairs of knickers, badly soiled, and a pair of brown tights. She returned them to the sack and replaced the bundle beneath the bench.

She glanced at her watch. It was almost an hour since she left the car. She'd stayed too long. Dragging the ladder back to the block with the holes, she climbed to the top then pulled herself up and out through the roof light.

The industrial estate was deserted: no cars, no vans, no people. Railway signals and floodlights were reflected on the surface of the canal and, beyond the dark oily water, a train of wagons rumbled and clattered through the marshaling yards. She turned and looked down the road that wound like a necklace of orange lights through the estate. There was no sign of a white van.

Samantha stepped over the bridge of girders, grabbed the handrail around the silo platform and vaulted over it. Seconds later she was emerging through the yard gates and sprinting for the car.

*   *   *

Hugh Dixon crossed the deserted dual carriageway then headed up the familiar road through the area of old terrace housing. He'd not bothered with his run the previous night. He'd had no pent-up energy to release. Yesterday afternoon with Emma had been mindblowing, and the nagging desire that normally haunted every waking moment had been assuaged.

He crossed the road without checking for traffic. Emma's eyes, her smile, her breathless little moans, those curving expanses of silky skin, were still vividly real. Nothing was the same any more. His life had changed. He was obsessed. Was this, he wondered, what they meant by being in love?

Terraced houses gave way to nondescript inter-war semis. He was running exceptionally well tonight, moving at a brisk pace now he'd cleared the rise. And he was certain that this elation, this euphoric feeling of wellbeing, flowed from his relationship with Emma.

Relationship? Yes, perhaps he could start calling it that now. They'd spent some fabulous hours together, she'd delighted him by becoming even more uninhibited, and she'd promised to call him before the end of the week. Her husband was the problem: a vague presence in the background that made things difficult for her. Hugh could understand that. He'd have to be patient and play his cards right until she become as besotted with him as he was with her. They might have a real life together then.

The rhythmic padding of his trainers on the moonlit pavement, the steady beating of his heart, helped him to lose himself in his thoughts. He'd run these streets so often the landmarks no longer made an impression on him. He didn't even realize he was passing the school.

And then the pavement ended and he was running along the side of the road that dipped gently between open fields. No longer hidden behind rooftops, a full moon, low on the horizon, shone down on ripening corn and cast long shadows across the tarmac.

Hugh didn't notice the moonlight. He was savouring the memory of Emma with her white satin slip nicked up around her waist and her plump thighs spread across that Chinese rug. He didn't hear the distant whine of a starter, an engine clattering into life, the rumble of a van accelerating down the road behind him.

The impact seemed no more than a jolt, as if someone had bumped into him on a crowded pavement. It was only when he was sprawling in the grass and nettles that the enormity of the pain raped his consciousness. He heard brakes squeal, a van door slam, heavy boots run along the road then brush through long grass. He felt powerful hands grabbing him, dragging him back to the road.

'No!' Hugh screamed. 'Christ, no! My leg; it's broken. Get an ambulance. Get . . . an . . . ambulance.'

The man ignored him, went on dragging him out of the long grass.

'Jesus, no. Don't. Don't move me.'

'Bastard!' Jack Slater snarled. 'Fornicating bastard. You've been having it off with my missus.'

Hugh moaned through a haze of pain, realized it was Emma's husband. She must have told him. Christ, what a Neanderthal! How could Emma be married to someone like that?

'Haven't you?' Jack demanded.

Hugh felt a fist smash into his face, tried to lift his arms to protect himself, but he couldn't move or feel them. 'I'm sorry,' he moaned, then coughed as blood began to fill his throat.

'Sorry?' Jack roared. 'Fucking sorry? You're going to find out what sorry means.'

'Please,' Hugh moaned. 'No more. I've said I'm sorry. Please get me an ambulance.'

163

The fist smashed into his face again. 'How many times?'

'Times? I don't know,' Hugh sobbed, too distraught to lie. 'I didn't force her. She wanted it as much as me. She . . .'

'Dirty . . . little . . . bastard.' Jack Slater punctuated the words with more savage blows. He'd gashed his knuckles on teeth that were broken down to stumps, and his blood was splashing on to Hugh's face and dripping into his open mouth.

Jack heard a dog barking. The sound was coming from distant houses, but it alerted him to the need to get away before he was seen.

Sliding his hands under Hugh's arms, he dragged him, moaning, the twenty yards to the van. He opened the doors, lifted the limp body and threw it, face down, into the back. Hugh's legs were hanging down, twisted at crazy angles. When Jack grabbed them and heaved them inside, moans turned into screams. Jack reached for some heavy bar cutters lying near the wheel arch, then used them to batter the back of Hugh's head until the screaming stopped.

He slammed the doors shut, climbed into the driving seat and started the engine. Up ahead the road was deserted. He checked the rear view mirrors. There was no sign of move- ment along the mile or so of moonlit road behind him.

He'd done it and he'd not been seen. The

baby-faced bastard with the poncey antique shop wasn't going to make a fool of him any more.

CHAPTER ELEVEN

Betty Slater jerked upright, suddenly alert, straining to hear the faintest sound. She must have fallen asleep. It was impossible to stay awake all night, listening for Jack.

She heard it again; the scrape of a chair leg in the conservatory, a faint rustle of movement. The van door slamming, the clump of his booted feet down the side of the house, must have woken her without her having realized what the sounds were.

Betty swung her legs off the bed and groped for her bag and shoes. She'd been lying on the counterpane, fully dressed. She'd rested like that for the past week or more, ever since Jack had become really strange. Something about him had changed. He'd gone all quiet, always giving her those long cold stares, loathing her with his eyes. She sensed the danger in him. He'd been working all night, sleeping in the mornings, going back to the factory in the afternoons. He hardly touched his food and never spoke, just grunted.

But he'd not touched her since she'd threatened him with the Domestic Violence

Unit. She felt for her mobile phone now, her fingers moving over the glass top of the bedside cabinet. She heard another noise and her groping became more frantic until she suddenly realized she'd left it downstairs. Sweet Jesus, it was on the sofa! She hadn't picked it up when she'd switched off the television and come upstairs.

Betty could hear him clearly now. He'd left the downstairs conservatory, pushed his way past the table and chairs in the kitchen and stepped into the hall. Her heart was pounding.

She could hardly breathe. She couldn't let him find her. She had to hide.

She picked up her bag and shoes, then crept along the landing to the tiny bedroom at the front of the house. It contained a cupboard on top of a bulkhead above the stairs. She opened the cupboard doors, lifted out some empty suitcases, and climbed inside, still clutching her bag and shoes. There were no handles on her side of the doors, so she clawed at the edges with her fingernails, somehow managing to pull them almost shut. She knelt there, bag pressed against her chest, her hair tangling with the wire branches of the Christmas tree. Fear was intensifying her need for the toilet, and she was squeezing her thighs together to stop the dribbling.

'Betty!' The voice filtered up from the sitting room. 'Get down here. I want you. I want to talk to you.'

She knelt there, silent, trembling, squeezing her thighs; listening to him prowling around.

'Betty!' He was yelling up the stairs now.

After a dozen thudding heartbeats she heard the slow pad of his feet on the stairs, and then, in a mocking sing-song voice, he chanted, 'I've got your mobile. You can't call the coppers.'

The footsteps stopped on the half landing.

'He's dead, Betty. Your fancy man's dead.'

She pressed her shaking thighs together, trying desperately to stop the flow. Her pants and tights were wet against her skin. She held her breath.

'You're a lying bitch, Betty.'

She heard the creak of the loose stair tread. He was moving up the second flight. His breathing was audible now: deep and laboured, as if he was struggling to keep himself under control.

'He couldn't remember how many times he'd fucked you, Betty. He told me you'd wanted it as much as he had.' And then his voice became a barely audible whine as he asked, 'Why did you lie to me, Betty? Why did you say you hadn't let him fuck you?'

She heard him climb a couple more steps.

'I've killed the bastard, Betty.' His voice was a threatening growl. 'Only question is, what do I do with you? I mean, what bloke wants to dip his wick in dirty oil?' He let out a bitter laugh. 'Fact is, Betty, I just can't believe it. Handsome young bloke like that wanting to screw a fat-arsed cow like you. Christ, I could only manage it when I was desperate, and I was duty bound.'

She heard him round the top of the landing and kick their bedroom door open.

'Betty!' he roared. 'Come here, you filthy slag.'

A light switch clicked, he muttered something she couldn't catch, then began to move closer.

'Where are you, bitch?'

A door crashed open.

She held her breath. He was moving around the big front bedroom now, muttering to himself.

Retracing his steps, he crossed the landing and approached her hiding place.

'Betty!'

Her pounding heart lurched.

The door to the tiny bedroom squealed open then crashed against the doors of her cupboard. Rigid with fright, Betty lost what little control she had over her bladder, felt the hot wetness spurt between her thighs and wash down her legs.

A switch clicked and light gleamed through the gap between the cupboard doors.

'Betty!' His voice was deafeningly close.

'Bitch,' he muttered. 'Fat cheating slag's buggered off.'

She heard his footsteps receding down the

landing, the slam of the bathroom door. After what seemed like an age, she caught the faint hiss of the shower. She knew this was her chance. She pushed the cupboard doors open, wincing as they thudded against the bedroom door, and climbed out. Clutching her bag and shoes, she crept around the landing and down the stairs.

Something hard and sharp pricked the sole of her foot and she stumbled against the telephone table. Glancing down, she saw the shattered remains of her mobile phone.

Betty limped into the kitchen, heading for the back door. When she entered the conservatory she saw Jack's clothes heaped on some black bin liners he'd spread over the tiles. Everything was there; shirt, vest, pants, jeans, socks, his huge boots on top; and everything was soaked with blood.

Skirting the gruesome pile, she stepped out into the night and ran down the side of the house. After crossing the road she glanced back. Lights blazed in every empty room.

She continued to run in her stockinged feet until she rounded the corner at the newsagent's. The windows had been covered, and someone had sprayed 'Paki Bastards' across the chipboard sheets. She leant against them while she pulled on her shoes. Then, wet pants and tights cold against her skin, she began to half-walk, half-run, down the hill towards the town.

A police helicopter was droning overhead, its searchlight drifting across rooftops, and she could hear the faint sounds of shouts and chanting. On the rise beyond the ring road, shops, a garage and whole streets of houses were burning, the flames sending up showers of sparks into the darkness.

She shivered. Everything was falling apart: her marriage, the town, the country. She hadn't realized how bad things had become over the past few weeks. She'd had her own problems, been too preoccupied to read newspapers or concentrate on television broadcasts. It made her situation worse. This was no time for a woman to be running away from her home without the support and protection of a man.

*   *   *

Betty began to run as she neared the shop. If Jack had hurt that quiet decent man she'd go straight to the police.

Turning out of a street that sloped down to the main road, she ran past a dress shop, a travel agent's, the Angel and Royal pub, then slowed as she approached his shop, trying to regain her breath. Windows and door were covered over with the rough plywood sheets she'd seen in his workshop.

She hammered on the door with her fists, then stepped back into the road and looked up at the first floor windows. Nothing moved behind the small panes of glass, but she could see the faint glow of a lamp.

Alarm escalated into a panicky fear. Betty forgot the cold wetness between her legs, the chill of the night air through her silk blouse. She ran back to the door and pounded it harder.

She heard the squeal of a sash window lifting and stepped back to the edge of the pavement. Adam Turner was leaning over the cill.

'You're OK!' she gasped. 'Thank God you're OK.'

'Why shouldn't I be OK?'

'Jack said he'd killed you.'

'Jack?'

'My husband. He said he'd murdered you.'

Adam Turner laughed. 'Why on earth would he want to do that?'

'Can I come in?' Betty asked. 'I need to come in.'

'Sure. Just a minute.'

The window slid shut. Seconds later chinks of light appeared around the boards protecting the windows and door, bolts were sliding, a key turned in the lock and the door swung open.

Betty stepped inside, holding her bag, blinking in the bright light of a couple of huge chandeliers. For the first time in days she felt safe. She began to shake with relief and delayed shock, and suddenly realized how cold

171

and wet she was.

'Hey, you're as white as a ghost.' Adam Taylor's voice sounded concerned. He dragged a sheet from a chair. 'Sit down. I'll get you a drink and you can tell me . . .'

'I can't sit down.' Betty's teeth were chattering now. 'I wet myself. I'm soaking. I'll spoil your chair.'

'Wet yourself?'

'When he came in. I hid in a cupboard and he kept yelling for me, saying he'd killed you. I thought he was going to kill me. I was so scared I . . .'

'Come upstairs.' He gestured for her to go through to the workshop.

'No. You lead the way. My skirt's soaked through at the back. I don't want you to see me in this state.'

Adam nodded, went ahead of her, began to climb the stone steps that were let into the workshop wall.

He glanced back at her. 'Why on earth would your husband want to kill me?'

'He thought we were having an affair.'

Adam laughed. 'An affair?'

'He knew I was coming to see you about the desk. I don't know how, but every time I came he knew I'd been and how long I'd stayed. And he's consumed by this crazy jealousy.'

He led her into his flat-cum-storeroom. A book lay over the arm of a wing chair. On a small table next to the chair stood an ornate

172

gold lamp with a black shade and a whisky bottle and glass.

'Can I have a bath and wash my clothes?' Betty blurted the words out.

'You could have a shower. There isn't a bath.' He gestured across the big room that was filled with gleaming antiques.

'No. You go first,' she said hastily. 'Have you got an old coat; something I could wear while my clothes dry?'

'I'll find you a bathrobe. That OK?' He was being propelled along by the woman's distress, her desperate need, but, deep down, he was feeling a little alarmed, a little used. He hardly knew her. She'd come banging on his door in the middle of the night, saying her crazy husband wanted to murder him. The situation was bizarre.

He led her into a small utility room containing a washing machine, a hand basin and a shower cubicle. 'I won't be a second. I'll just get the robe.'

Betty opened the cubicle door and peered inside. There was soap and shower gel in a tray. It was hardly luxurious, but it was neat and scrupulously clean, like the workshop downstairs. She heard him enter the room and spun round, desperate to conceal the shaming wetness on the back of her skirt.

Adam handed her a dark-blue bathrobe, then held out a tumbler containing a generous measure of whisky. 'I thought you could use this.'

'Thanks,' she said, and then her face suddenly crumpled. 'God, I feel so dirty and ashamed. I don't know what I'd have done if you'd not . . .'

She was holding the robe in one hand, the whisky glass in the other, and her head was hanging down, her eyes unable to meet his concerned gaze. She was abject in her embarrassment, and plump shoulders under cream silk were heaving with silent sobs.

'Try not to be upset,' he said lamely. 'If someone broke in here and said he was going to kill me, I'd pee myself. Can you use the washing machine?'

Betty nodded dumbly and tried to choke back the sobs. Of course she could use the washer. What did he think she'd been doing for the past twenty years?

When she heard the door close she put the robe and glass on top of the washer, kicked off her shoes and began to undress, desperate to get out of the wet pants and tights.

Adam headed back to the island of light around the chair and retrieved his glass. He felt bemused by it all. He hardly knew the woman. She was just a customer with a passion for a little gilded desk. Her husband must be crazy.

The rhythmic beat of booted men running in step drifted up from the street. Adam went over to the front window. A dozen skinheads, dressed in army surplus battle fatigues, were running past the shop, heading out of town. He heard the wail of approaching sirens, the youths glanced back over their shoulders, then broke step as they doubled back and clattered under the archway at the side of the pub.

Cars sped past, lights flashing, sirens reaching a painful crescendo. When the noise had died away, the gang emerged from the opening, their guttural voices mocking and laughing at the police. They began to head back towards town and, after a dozen paces, fell in step again. Adam remained at the window, listening to the violent drumming of boots on tarmac until the chilling sound had faded away.

'What was all the noise?'

Adam turned. Betty Slater was standing at the adjoining window, peering down into the street. The blue robe reached almost to the floor. She'd wrapped it around her closely and pulled the belt tight, emphasizing her breasts and the dramatic sweep of her hips. With her hair pinned up and her cheeks pink from the shower she looked younger, more vulnerable. He couldn't imagine anyone wanting to hurt her.

'Skinhead gang trying to hide from the police,' he muttered. 'They've been smashing up all the newsagents and corner shops. I'm getting scared. The police seem to be losing control.'

'You're closer to the town centre,' she said. 'You see it happening here.'

'Can I get you some tea, or something to eat?'

She shook her head. 'It's almost three o'clock. A drop more of that whisky would be nice though.'

'I'll join you,' he said.

He pulled a chair round to face his and gestured for her to sit down.

She made her way through the antiques to join him. 'You live amongst the stock then?'

'Got to. But it keeps changing so you don't get bored with the furniture. Where's your glass?'

'Sorry, I left it in the utility room.'

He smiled down at her and said, 'Sit there. I'll get it.'

The washing machine was churning her blue skirt around. Her tights and a shocking pink underskirt and lace trimmed pants were hanging over the shower screen: she must have washed them by hand. He saw the glass next to her bra and a neatly folded blouse on top of the washer. The sight of her underclothes disturbed him. He could have done without this intrusion. It was bad enough trying to control his thoughts about Emma, always reading late into the night because sleep endlessly evaded him. He picked up the glass and went back.

'You're surrounded by beautiful things,' she

said.

He handed her the glass, generously filled. The alcohol seemed to have calmed her. She wasn't trembling now. 'But nothing matches,' she went on.

Adam laughed and sat down, facing her.

Smiles and laughter transform his face, Betty mused. He's just a big, sweet, gentle bloke. Why had his wife let him go? And why hadn't she listened to her gran? Why hadn't she waited, got an education, relied on her brains rather than animal instincts and seething hormones.

She sipped at the whisky, then said, 'I'm sorry, putting you to all this trouble. It's just that when Jack said he'd killed you, I had to come and check. Thank God he was winding me up.'

'What are you going to do?'

She looked down at her hands. 'I've got to get away. Jack's dangerous. He's always been jealous and possessive, but he's crazy with it now. It started to get really bad when he won a big contract to supply blocks for some council job. He works all night, sleeps in the mornings, then goes back after lunch. But it's more than job worries. I can tell that. Something's eating away at him.'

She glanced up, her eyes searched Adam's face, then she said, 'His dad died about five years ago. He loved his dad. Big gentle bloke: soft as butter. Miner; got pneumoconiosis, coughed and gasped himself to death. Jack was devastated. It did something to him. I suppose that's when our marriage started going downhill.'

'How about you?' Adam asked, 'Do you have any family?'

Betty shook her head. 'No kids, thank God. I couldn't have coped with kids and Jack. My gran brought me up after my mother died: cancer, she was only thirty-eight. I never knew my dad. Gran died just after I got married. She never wanted me to marry Jack. She could see through him. I was just young and stupid.'

She sipped at the whisky and frowned. 'Funny, but Jack's mother warned me off him, too. I used to get on OK with his mum, but Jack seemed to want me to stay away from her. She married a retired baths manager soon after Jack's dad died, went down south to live on his council pension. Jack never bothered with her after that.'

Looking at her in the dim light, Adam was reminded again of the woman in Boucher's picture. Delicate features that came close to being beautiful, tiny hands with plump tapered fingers, tiny feet. It was pleasant having her in the flat, more pleasant than he'd care to admit, but their conversation had made him uneasy. A woman in trouble without friends or family: he didn't know how he was going to deal with the situation. 'Are you going to contact the police?' he asked.

'I'd have phoned them tonight if Jack hadn't found my mobile and smashed it. And when I got out of the house I had to find out if you were OK. Anyway, I was too embarrassed to contact anyone, the state I was in.'

They were silent while the drone of the police helicopter grew louder, then faded away as it cruised back towards the town.

'Could I stay the night?' Her eyes and her voice were begging him.

'You already have,' he laughed. 'It'll soon be getting light.'

'I'm sorry. I've messed you about, keeping you up like this.'

'I'd have stayed up anyway,' Adam said. 'I don't find it easy to get to sleep.'

'Is it because you've left your wife?' She sipped her drink.

'How did you know that?'

'You told me; one of the times I came to look at my desk. You told me no one else was involved, but you didn't really say why you'd left.'

Adam frowned down at his glass. Did she have to be so curious about his marriage?

'Weren't you getting on?'

'We got on pretty well. It's just that she's married to her job. She's the council's chief quantity surveyor.'

Betty looked impressed. 'Wish I'd had an education. Makes you more confident. You're always afraid educated people are laughing

179

at you.'

Adam couldn't imagine her being any more confident than she already was. 'If they were really educated, the last thing they'd do is laugh at you,' he said softly.

'I don't understand it,' Betty said, still probing. 'There's no one else and you got on OK, so why part?'

Can't she leave it alone? Adam fumed to himself, and his voice was terse when he said, 'We got on fine, like brother and sister.'

She raised her eyebrows and gave him a knowing look. 'That's marriage for you,' she laughed, and drained her glass.

'Care for another?'

She shook her head.

'You take the bed. I'll bunk down in the workshop.'

'Where is it; the bed I mean?' she asked.

Adam gestured towards the far wall.

Betty turned, saw a deeply carved gold and ivory creation with a circular canopy and powder-blue silk drapes. 'You sleep in that?'

'Until it's sold. I bought it a couple of months ago. Just finished refurbishing it.' He laughed at her faintly shocked expression. 'The mattress is new and the bedding's clean.'

They rose to their feet. She took her eyes from the bed and looked up at him.

'Don't go down to the workroom.'

'I really should,' Adam insisted, a little embarrassed. 'You're married; I'm married.'

'And I'm scared. I don't want to be alone tonight.'

Adam sighed. 'OK. You take the bed and I'll stretch out in this chair.'

'You don't find me attractive, is that it?'

'You must know that I do. What about Miss O'Mally on the chaise longue?' he reminded her.

Betty sniffed. 'I went to the library and found the picture in a book. She's just a fat woman lying face down on some pillows without any clothes on. I'm not as fat as that.'

'I never suggested you were.'

'But that's how you imagined me; big and fat with a huge backside.' She was becoming tearful. Jack's remarks had wounded her deeply. She'd thought this pleasant, cultured man fancied her, but he was rejecting her, too. It was all too much to bear.

'You're tired, you've been traumatized, and you're being silly,' Adam said reprovingly. 'You're not fat, you're not even plump, you're voluptuous. My wife is voluptuous. It's something I find very attractive in a woman. Most men don't care for skin and bone creatures.'

Betty stepped closer, reached out, took his hands, and placed them on her hips. 'Stay with me, then. Stay with me if you like what you see.'

Adam looked down into big brown eyes that were searching his. 'I'd feel guilty. My wife

181

would never dream of doing anything like that.'

'She'd never dream of doing it at all,' Betty whispered. 'Isn't that the trouble? How long has it been?'

Adam swallowed, moved his hands up the rough material of the robe until they were gently caressing the softness of her shoulders.

Betty began to move towards the bed. 'Hadn't you better switch off the lamp?'

'No,' he said breathlessly. 'I'd prefer to leave it on.'

CHAPTER TWELVE

Samantha Quest nudged Emma Turner. 'The man whose just come round the truck; do you recognize him?'

Emma peered through the windscreen towards the factory doors, squinting against the brightness of the summer morning. 'Mmm, no. Can't say I've seen him before.'

'He's a Barfield Barbarian,' Samantha said. 'The local rugger team. I don't suppose the borough architect's a member?'

'Old Stanley?' Emma giggled. 'I shouldn't think so. I can't imagine him scrumming down.'

They sat together, cool and comfortable in the Ferrari Modena, watching the huge block being rolled from the production line on to the back of a low-loader.

'Any reason why they'd cast deep holes in the blocks?' Samantha asked.

'Shouldn't be any voids,' Emma said. 'The design depends on the weight of the blocks to hold back the earth.'

'They're filled before the blocks leave the factory.'

Emma shrugged. 'They could be piping steam into the core of the blocks, pushing the temperature up to get a faster cure, but the chemicals they use should do that.'

'Why did you advise the borough architect to have the reinforcement in the blocks checked?'

'No particular reason. If the engineers were going on site to check the foundations, I thought they might as well run the metal detector over the blocks as well.'

'How about breakfast?' Samantha asked.

'I ought to get back to the office. And I've had breakfast.' Emma took a sideways glance at the woman in the ivory silk suit with its half-sleeved jacket and tight skirt. Glossy black hair, perfectly made-up eyes, red lips that matched her nails: it all looked very expensive, if a little unrestrained for her taste. But then, she reflected enviously, the woman had the youth and looks to carry it off.

Samantha was gazing towards the factory doors. The heat was making the air shimmer over the concrete beams and posts in the stack yard. She seemed deep in thought.

'Do you dine out a lot?' Emma asked, making conversation.

Samantha laughed. 'I never dine in.'

'Not even breakfast?'

'I don't even pour milk on corn flakes. I couldn't boil an egg. I stop at tea and instant coffee.'

'You're kidding?'

'It's true,' Samantha insisted, still laughing. 'You should try it. It's very liberating, and you soon find the best places to dine.'

'They've finished the re-measure on the rock,' Emma said, becoming serious. 'I told you about that?'

Samantha nodded. The entire block had emerged from the factory now and was progressing slowly along the rollers towards the cab of the truck. She was thinking about vertical shafts and dirty underwear in a plastic sack, trying to make some sense of it all.

'It's confirmed the overpayment,' Emma went on. 'In fact, we've got to claw back so much in this month's valuation it's going to be embarrassing. I'm worried about it.'

'Worried?' Samantha took her mind off concrete blocks, turned in her seat and gave Emma her full attention.

God, the woman's eyes, Emma thought. Witch's eyes: burning right into your soul, illuminating all its dark secret places. She swallowed hard, then said, 'Worried it might result in them threatening me, like they threatened Stanley Jackson. I've got a beautiful young daughter, too.'

'I'd go for it,' Samantha said. 'Deduct the overpayment. The rock business has nothing to do with the threats. Whoever made the threats is worried about these blocks.'

'No one's queried the blocks,' Emma protested.

'The engineers were going to look them over while they were checking the foundations and the men who were going to do the checking both reported sick. It's these blocks.'

'What if you're wrong?'

'Trust me, it's the blocks, not the rock,' Samantha insisted. 'Look, measuring and calculating payment for what's done is your responsibility, right?'

'In a word, yes.' Emma said.

'Then do your job. Correct the valuation, deduct the over-payment from the . . . what did you call it?'

'Certificate,' Emma prompted.

'And let me know what happens. If you're not threatened, we'll know for sure it's the blocks.'

'*If* I'm not threatened?' There was a note of outrage in Emma's voice.

Samantha laughed. 'I promise you won't be. We can't just do nothing. If the deduction provokes a response, I'll deal with the

185

problem.'

Emma looked worried and unconvinced.

'Trust me.' Samantha smiled and squeezed her hand. 'Now, how about breakfast? Watching big men sweating over concrete blocks has given me an appetite.'

Emma laughed despite herself. 'I've told you, I've had breakfast.'

'Have another. I know a hotel where the chef does poached-eggs-on-haddock to die for.' Samantha started the Ferrari. She accelerated away from the wharf, cruised past the factory as sedately as she could, then roared up the winding estate road, heading back to town.

*   *   *

Marcus was surprised, but not particularly flattered, at having been told to travel in the ministerial car rather than one of the Range Rover escorts. Things were getting worse by the day; public fear and unrest, sporadic outbreaks of rioting. Security had to be uppermost in politicians' minds now.

Armed officers peered down from every bridge. Patrol cars were parked at the crest of every slip road. The limousine was surging up the motorway, its heavy bullet proofing making it unusually silent, despite the speed.

'Where the devil are we?' the minister demanded tetchily.

'Just moving up the A1, skirting Barfield. We'll be in Leeds in about thirty minutes, minister,' explained Pogmore, the senior civil servant organizing the trip.

'Barfield,' the minister muttered, thoughtfully. 'Isn't that where half the councillors went down for corruption?'

'I don't think it was half, Minister. A few of them got their expenses claims wrong.'

'You make it sound trifling, Pogmore. I don't consider a gang of socialist tykes on the make a trifling matter.'

'Quite so, Minister. But we have to look inside the House for the really big scandals, don't we?'

'Inside the House?' The minister sounded mystified.

'House of Commons, Minister. Those hospital contracts: group of Members taking a cut of the profits from the contractors? Select Committee is due to report soon, but it looks as if they've shared a million-pound backhander between them. Surely you remember it, Minister?'

The Home Secretary, grunted and lapsed into a scowling silence.

Marcus smiled to himself. Years of practice had made Pogmore a master of the obsequious put-down.

'Were you happy with your briefing, Minister?' Pogmore asked.

'Briefing was comprehensive enough, but

the situation's serious. I see you put troops on the streets in Bradford and they killed thirty rioters.'

'Killed six, Minister,' Pogmore corrected gently. 'Twenty-four injured, some seriously.'

'Kept that out of the media: sending the troops in, I mean.'

'Dressed them in police riot gear,' Pogmore said. 'But that's Marcus's territory. His department organized it.'

The minister leant forward so he could see Marcus. 'Not good killing Muslims on the streets, Marcus, even if they are rioting. Only excites the blighters and makes more terrorists.'

'What do we do, Minister? Let them riot?'

Pogmore winced. Security chaps had no diplomacy. The minister had to be handled more carefully than that. Best thing was to be subtle and take the piss out of him gently.

'You should go for the skinheads and the fascists,' the Home Secretary went on. 'The lunatics who are torching the mosques, fomenting all this trouble. Things would calm down then.'

'More than fifty white rioters were arrested, Minister. And the local police are making headway with the arson cases.'

'Arrested, not killed. Only Muslims were killed. Their community leaders are going to give me a hammering about that over lunch, Marcus. The local Labour MP is making a

188

meal of it, and the ethnic vote swings these marginal seats.'

After they'd ridden in silence for another mile, the Home Secretary turned back to Marcus and asked, 'How's the tube bombing investigation going?'

'We're pretty sure the bombers were home grown and came from Birmingham.'

'It's been almost two weeks. Is that all you can tell me: "A couple of Brummies did it"?' The minister's voice was scathing.

'When you only find a few charred body parts and you're not sure whether they belong to the bombers or the victims, you don't have much to go on, Minister.'

'I thought you were intelligence gatherers?' the minister snorted, then glanced at Pogmore, 'What's the budget for MI5 now?'

'Three hundred million, Minister. That includes the additional allocation for recruitment voted through in January.'

The minister glared at Marcus. 'For three hundred million, Marcus, I'd expect the security services to buy enough intelligence to be able to act before the event.'

'A strong team's being put together, Minister. I'm meeting the last recruit tonight. If she'll join we'll be formidable.'

'She?'

'Quest. Samantha Quest.'

'Didn't you try and persuade the Foreign Secretary to talk to the Russians and the

Americans about her acting as courier for an American national?'

Marcus nodded.

The minister laughed. 'Must say, you've got the cheek of the devil.'

'I won't bore you with the details, Minister, but it was a way of getting her back into Eastern Europe and the Middle East.'

The minister smirked at Pogmore, then gave Marcus a knowing look. 'I'm told she's extremely beddable.'

'She's the most sexually attractive woman I've ever met,' Marcus said.

'Really!' the minister was grinning now. 'Sexy but not beautiful: bit of a tart? Is that what you're trying to say, Marcus?'

Marcus shook his head, suddenly feeling defensive. 'Beautiful too, Minister, and very elegant.'

'Haldane at the Foreign Office thinks she's a psychopath.'

'She's ruthless, determined, mind like a razor, has a photographic memory, but I certainly wouldn't describe her as a psychopath,' Marcus said.

'I'm told she took a dreadful revenge on some terrorists who murdered her sister: hunted down and killed all the members of the group.'

'Almost all, Minister. The Americans killed two and there's one still standing.'

The Home Secretary sniffed reprovingly.

'You'll know that the Russian Minister of the Interior presented her with a gift from a grateful Russian people. That can hardly endear her to us.'

'She exposed the group that masterminded the last wave of Moscow bombings,' Marcus said. 'Identified them all. Russian police took the credit, and it did a lot for the president in election year. They'd every reason to be grateful.'

'Perhaps old Grazyev, their Interior Minister, wanted to get his leg over,' Pogmore suggested.

The minister chuckled. 'I hardly think so. He'd have known how she got the information on the bombers. Duncan at MI6 showed me photographs. Shot 'em full of drugs, put a wire noose round their genitals and plugged it into the public power supply. Slow electrical castration. Burning was dreadful. Just looking at the pictures made strong men cross their legs and weep.' He laughed. 'She's not a woman you'd sleep comfortably with after seeing images like that.'

The minister glanced from a queasy looking Pogmore to a grinning Marcus. 'I'm told she was trained by the Israeli secret service.'

'You've been well informed, Minister.'

'She's not one of us, Marcus.' The minister's voice had become low and vaguely threatening.

'She's a British subject. Had full clearance

to the highest level. Has an outstanding record with MI6.'

'I don't mean that. I'm saying she doesn't understand the rules of the game: the unwritten rules. She could set a lot of hares running; embarrass our sort of people. I'm sure you know what I'm saying, Marcus.'

'Of course, Minister. But, like you said, the situation's dire and I must recruit the best.'

'Be it on your head.'

'Is a state of emergency to be declared?' Marcus asked.

'PM's going to announce it in the House on Friday. Come into effect at midnight.'

Marcus felt a surge of relief. Security services would still get the arse-kickings, but at least their hands were being untied.

The minister stared out at the passing landscape. 'Where are we now?'

'Approaching Leeds, Minister. We'll be there in about five minutes. The meeting with civic and ethnic minority leaders is scheduled for twelve-thirty.'

'I'm not looking forward to this, Pogmore.'

'We can pull you out if things become difficult, Minister. I deliberately kept the timetable tight. The meeting in Bradford is at three. I'll just announce that you've got to move on, and we'll leave.'

*   *   *

'You look absolutely ravishing, Sam.'

'Why, thank you, Marcus.' Samantha let him take her black satin evening coat and winced when he casually tossed it over the back of a chair.

'Nice hotel suite,' she said.

'Not bad for Leeds.'

'Not bad for anywhere.'

Samantha took in the starkly elegant room. Carpet, drapes and walls were different shades of off-white, lit by clusters of tiny lights scattered over the ceiling. An extravagant display of flowers stood on a low glass table that ran the length of a white leather sofa. A glass-topped dining table had been laid for two. In an alcove, a desk was strewn with papers, and a laptop, its screen glowing, lay open on the blotter.

'You look good in the tux,' she said.

Marcus laughed. 'I knew you'd be well turned out, so I thought I ought to try my best.' He looked her over. 'Beautiful dress, by the way. Such a vivid red; and that flouncy skirt, what's it made of?'

'Layers of silk ribbons. It's a Dell' Acqua original: twenties retro.'

'Bit like a grass skirt?'

'Not really, there's silk under the ribbons.'

He let his eyes range over her again, sighed, then muttered more to himself than to her, 'Ravishing; utterly ravishing.'

She watched while he rotated a bottle in an

ice bucket; pleased she'd overwhelmed him with her appearance, despising herself for being pleased, for attaching the slightest value to his opinions.

'Champagne?' he asked. 'Should be chilled now.'

'Champagne is fine.'

He deftly popped the cork into a napkin, poured a couple of glasses, and handed one over.

'The food's being specially prepared, so I've ordered for both of us. Hope you don't mind. We're having . . .'

'Don't tell me,' Samantha interrupted. 'Just let it unfold as a pleasant surprise.'

While she crossed over to the white sofa and sat down, he lifted a phone on the desk and told the chef his guest had arrived.

He didn't join her on the sofa, just leant against the desk, sipped champagne, and made no attempt to conceal the fact that he was enjoying looking at her.

After a while he said, 'Why the clothes, Sam? You always wear such beautiful things. I mean, you don't come across as the kind of woman who'd be all that bothered about what she wore.'

Samantha didn't like his question. Thinking about it too much could only draw her into the dark places nightmares came from. In a vague and uncertain way, she sensed that, for her, being scrupulously clean, being immaculately dressed, was a ritualized cleansing of guilt and sin. She shuddered. Perhaps it was an endless washing away of her victims' blood.

Samantha looked down at red nails that exactly matched the colour of her dress, and said evasively, 'Clothes are my shield against the chaos, a way of bringing some order into my life. Does that make sense, Marcus?'

'Not to me,' he laughed.

'Surely your wife likes decent clothes?'

'She's not really fashion conscious,' Marcus said. 'Jumper, tweed skirt, green wellies during the day, trousers in the evening, frock if we go out. She breeds sheep: country girl at heart: bishop's daughter.'

Samantha looked at him, strangely comforted by the picture he'd painted, and struggling to hide a smile.

'Couldn't afford to dress her like that, though,' Marcus admitted, nodding at the red dress. 'Just sent the girls to Felsham Ladies' College; costing me an arm and a leg.'

'How are your beautiful daughters?'

'Getting more beautiful by the day,' he said, then added gallantly, 'Getting more like their mother.'

There was a knock on the door and a couple of dinner-jacketed waiters wheeled in a trolley covered with silverware.

Marcus beckoned her over to the table, helped her into her chair, and the meal began.

Only Marcus could make dinner for two

seem so formal, she mused. And the chef's creations were exquisitely prepared and served, but minimalist, like the decor. She was still feeling peckish when the coffee and chocolates were brought in.

'I presume it's safe to talk in here?' she asked.

'No one knows who we are and I had the room swept before you arrived. It's as safe as it gets.'

During the meal they'd skirted around the issues, Marcus deftly controlling the conversation and avoiding questions he didn't want to answer. Now he had to come to the point.

'I want you back, Sam. I'm going to organize the Russian trip, but I need a little more time. Until I do, couldn't you operate in Britain? There's plenty of pruning needs to be done here. If you wanted, you could base yourself in the North and hardly venture into London.'

She eyed him over the rim of a delicate little yellow and gold coffee cup. 'And when the issue of the last man's been resolved?'

'Once we've got to grips with the situation at home you could transfer back to MI6, if that's what you wanted. They'd probably assign you to Eastern Europe, the Middle East; depends how things develop.'

She sipped her coffee. She didn't want this. She was comfortable in her new life, beginning to find it almost pleasant. There was sufficient to interest her and keep her from vegetating in the nondescript Yorkshire town, and investment income from a couple of inheritances was funding her passion for fine clothes. Problem was, Marcus would never arrange for her to deal with the last man if she didn't return, and she couldn't rely on the Russians holding an American national indefinitely.

She had to have closure. It was vital to her mental well-being.

'What delightful little Pharaoh feet you've got,' Marcus said wistfully, gazing down through the glass table. Samantha's eyebrows lifted. 'I'm sorry?'

'Pharaoh feet: like the feet in Egyptian tomb paintings. The second and third toes project as much as the first. They're exquisite.'

Samantha began laughing. 'Didn't know you were into feet, Marcus. How does your wife feel about your naughty little foot fetish? Does she like having her toes sucked?'

She was surprised to see him blushing. 'She used to quite enjoy it, but the years roll on . . .' He was laughing despite himself.

Samantha wrinkled her nose. 'Don't suppose it's the same after wearing green wellies and chasing sheep all day?' she said, and began to laugh helplessly.

Marcus threw his head back and laughed with her.

For the first time she felt a warmth, a

camaraderie, towards him. The revelation of his silly little sexual preference had made this aloof, patrician man seem human; and he was mature enough to laugh at himself.

'I need your answer tonight, Sam,' he said, suddenly serious. 'After all the extra funding we've had, I've got to show results.'

Samantha frowned at him over the remains of their meal. 'You'll make the arrangements for me to deal with Nasari?'

'Like I said, it'll take me a little time, but I will.'

'By Christmas?'

'At the very latest.'

'And until then I operate mainly in the north of England?'

'If that's what you want.'

'OK, Marcus, I'll run with it.'

He smiled at her, his body relaxing with relief. Rising from the table, he went over to the paper-strewn desk in the alcove and brought back a manila envelope, its flap secured by green string wrapped around metal tags. He unwound the string and shook the contents on to the table.

'Here's your letter of engagement.' He slid a paper over.

Samantha ran her eyes over the text, then glanced up at him. 'The pay scale's not mentioned.'

'It's a post and salary at the Head of Department's discretion. He pointed to the last paragraph of the letter. 'The figure's there, I think.'

'You should have mentioned the salary earlier,' Samantha muttered.

'Would it have made any difference?'

'Mmm, not really, but it's generous. How many agents are you recruiting in this way?'

'Twelve; seven with me and five with another section head.'

'Do I know any of them?'

'I doubt it,' Marcus said, then hurried on, 'This is your MI5 identification.' He handed her a small wallet. 'And this identifies you as an officer with the new Serious Crimes Unit. You're not, but you could find it useful if you're forced to deal with the police.'

He shook the envelope again and a small booklet tumbled out. 'This explains the Emergency Powers legislation. Read it, try and follow the guidance, but, above all, be discreet. Always make sure your actions can't be traced back to the government or the department.'

'They're going to declare a state of emergency, then?'

'On Friday, I gather. The powers we get under the legislation start midnight Friday. OK?'

Samantha nodded. 'My role, Marcus? How do I figure in your scheme of things?'

He strode back to the desk and returned with a plastic wallet. 'There are images of all known domestic terrorists and suspected terrorists; racketeers dealing in drugs, passport and credit card scams, prostitution and whatever, on this disk. They've been given a priority rating. Some are marked for disposal. That's your job.'

'Don't you want them for interrogation?'

'They've been under surveillance, for years in some cases, and some have been pulled in for questioning more than once. We've decided a quick pruning is the best thing, just eliminate the bastards, cripple their organizations. If we arrest them there'll be endless trouble from civil rights activists. We're not taking prisoners, Sam. We're not lining lawyer's pockets.'

Samantha met his gaze for a few moments, then raised a quizzical eyebrow.

'We've been thorough,' he added, sensing her reservations. 'Scrupulously careful. The people marked for disposal represent a certain terrorist threat.'

'And what about the ones given a lower priority?'

'So long as it's covert, so long as your actions can't be traced back, you've got a free hand. Dammit, these people are mired in crime: prostitution, drugs, extortion. They're already under threat of death from one another. And remember, you're not concerned with surveillance. Other people have been assigned to that, and you'll be kept informed of developments.'

Marcus passed over the envelope and Samantha began to slide the documents and other items inside.

'What about the local police?' she asked.

'Best avoided. The chief constables are edgy. They didn't like it when the Serious Crimes Unit was set up and they like soldiers in police uniforms even less. They think their autonomy's being threatened. And they can have divided loyalties: there's as much networking outside the force as there is within it. You could be compromised.' He gave her a meaningful look.

'Who's acting as armourer?'

'Armourer?'

'If I need equipment: something special, an Uzi maybe, or a night scope?'

'An Uzi! Christ, Sam, this is Britain, not Afghanistan.'

'I could take you to places where you wouldn't know the difference,' she muttered. 'You can't have it all ways, Marcus. You want results; I'll need equipment.'

He retrieved the emergency powers booklet and jotted a phone number inside the back cover. 'Phone this number, day or night, and ask for Ulrich. Tell her what you want and she'll organize it.' He began to slide the booklet back to her, then, remembering something, pulled it back and added another number. 'These people run an ambulance service if you want a body collecting. They're not organized to give you back-up, but they can dispose of bodies.'

'What about back up?'

He shook his head. 'There isn't any. You're on your own.'

'What if it's crime, not terrorism. Something big?'

'Discuss it with me if you have the time, otherwise use your initiative. Don't contact the police or the Serious Crimes Unit. You'll compromise security.'

Samantha took the booklet, slid it inside the manila envelope and wound the string around the tags. She already felt daunted and manipulated. Marcus had got what he wanted on the promise of Nasari's death, but she wasn't ready. Her mental state was too precarious for her to return. She sighed. At least Marcus was honourable: most of the section heads would have expected sex as part of the deal.

He looked tired. There was nothing more they could say to one another, and Samantha had a sudden craving to be nursing a double whisky in the tiny house she called home. She rose from the table and began to drift towards the door. Marcus helped her on with her coat.

'Give it your best, Sam. Just take them out quietly, without anyone realizing how it happened. We don't want to overexcite the crazy buggers and end up making more terrorists. And above all, be discreet.' He opened the door.

Samantha stepped out into the corridor, laughing softly. 'Don't worry, Marcus,' she said. 'I'll be discreet. I won't tell anyone what a kinky little toe-sucker you are.'

CHAPTER THIRTEEN

Jack Slater was struggling with the final invoice to Bartlets. Bookwork had never been his thing, and trembling fingers were making his handwriting spidery, almost illegible. Betty usually typed the invoices, but she'd gone, the bitch.

Less than an hour ago, old Frank had told him the surveillance cameras had picked her up at three that morning, hammering on the antique shop door, and the video showed the owner letting her in. It was crazy; absolutely bloody crazy. He'd driven the shop owner to the factory not long after midnight, butchered the fornicating bastard and had him sealed inside the last of the blocks before three. Some stupid bugger at the station must have got the videotapes mixed up.

Jack ran a finger around his collar. Thinking was as difficult as writing; the woolliness in his head, the incessant throbbing pain. Everything was sliding out of control.

He tossed the pen down, leant back in the

swivel chair and allowed his eyes to focus beyond the office doorway, on the water tanks, the network of pipes, the huge drum of the mixer, and the now empty production line. It would all be humming again tomorrow: urgent police order for concrete roadblocks; said he'd got to keep on supplying until they told him to stop. Nice little earner, and simple, too. He could leave the foreman and the new gang to get on with it while he took a couple of weeks off, got himself together again, maybe saw the doctor about the headaches and chest pains.

The sudden sound of a hand pounding on metal startled him. He rose, walked out of the office and over to the huge sliding doors. He began to lift the locking bar, thought better of it, and growled, 'Who is it?'

'Manos. Ramiz Manos. Vrakimi sent me with a bonus, a thank-you for what you've done.'

Jack lifted the bar, slid the doors apart and looked out into the floodlit yard. The little Albanian was holding a bottle of whisky in one hand, an envelope in the other. Jack stepped aside, Manos entered, and he heaved the doors shut.

The little man handed Jack the envelope. 'Vrakimi wanted you to have this. He's grateful. It's been good working with you, getting rid of all those dead whores.' He laughed, his teeth big and white, then nudged Jack with his elbow. 'I thought we should have

204

a drink together, wash away that smell you can almost taste, eh?' He waved the bottle and laughed again.

Jack did his best to smile back. He didn't want this. He wanted to go home, see if Betty had come back, find some aspirin for his headache. He made a pathetic attempt at sounding jovial: 'Come on through to the office. I'll get a couple of paper cups.'

Hunger and tiredness made Jack vulnerable to the alcohol. Thinking became even more difficult. His body ached to be in a bed, his mind craved the oblivion of sleep.

The Albanian eyed him shrewdly, then flashed his big strong teeth in an easy smile and said, 'One more, Jack, just one more. Then I go and see what those idle whores are doing.'

'No more.' Jack waved his hand. 'I've got to drive home. Got to . . .'

'Where's your cup?' The little man demanded. 'You've lost it. I'll get you another.'

He stood up, moved behind Jack, heading towards the coffee percolator and the pile of paper cups. Suddenly he turned, slid a lead truncheon from his sleeve and brought it down hard on the back of Jack's head. Jack cursed and tried to rise. Panicking, Manos delivered more blows until the curly black hair was matted with blood and ruptured flesh. Jack's massive shoulders sagged. He slumped off the chair and his long legs slithered inside the kneehole of the desk.

Manos tugged the envelope from Jack's back pocket, then dragged him out of the office into the gloom of the factory. The Albanian had watched Jack operate the plant many times, and was familiar with its workings. He got the gantry crane over, lowered the hook and slid it under Jack's belt. Operating the controls, he hoisted Jack's limp body, transported it over the mouth of the mixing drum, and lowered it inside.

He climbed up to a high platform, threw a lever and brought the drum almost to the pouring position, setting the rim at what he judged to be a little below Jack's knee level.

Manos peered inside. Jack's body was draped over one of four slatted metal vanes, each the size of a park bench, that were welded to the drum to agitate the mixing concrete. Groaning now, Jack was groping with his hands, trying to get a purchase on the curving metal.

The little Albanian stepped inside, tugged the hook from Jack's belt, then scrambled out and set the drum rotating.

Supported by the shelf-like metal vane, Jack's body swung gently upwards, then suddenly slid free and dropped almost ten feet to the floor of the drum. Dark eyes glittering, teeth bared in a satisfied smile, Manos watched Jack's body tumble around until, caught by another metal vane, it was hoisted aloft again.

Arrogant English bastard: who the hell did he think he was, yelling at him, treating him like the village idiot?

Manos climbed down to the factory floor, returned the crane to the end of its track, then went into the office. He glanced around. No blood had been spilled on the desk or the floor. Jack's thick mane of curly black hair had soaked it up.

He wiped the whisky bottle with the sleeve of his jacket, picked up the cup he'd used, and returned to the entrance doors.

He took a last look down the vast metal enclosure. Up in the gloom the huge drum was turning slowly, and every few seconds Jack's body thudded down, the sound imparting a sinister rhythm to the rumble of the machinery.

*   *   *

Samantha watched a swarthy little man emerge from the factory, strut across the floodlit parking area, and climb into a black Mercedes. The clatter of the starter echoed across the distance, then the big car swung out on to the road and headed off through the industrial estate.

She left the loading area alongside the wharf and kept the Mercedes' rear lights in view, her own lights switched off. At the junction with the ring road, the Mercedes turned left, heading towards Barfield. Samantha turned on her lights and followed.

She'd made a detour on her way back from Leeds, intent on taking a look at the factory. When she'd seen the car parked in the yard she'd decided to watch and wait; mull over her conversation with Marcus.

Her compliance was essential. It was the only way she could be sure of removing the threat posed by the last member of the group. She'd killed members of his family, his comrades; inflicted so much pain, extracted so much retribution. Once free, and she'd no doubt he would get free, Nasari would hound her to the grave, become the unseen assassin, forever stalking her.

Could she keep her part of the bargain? Could she go back? She wouldn't know until she tried, but she had the gravest doubts. She'd had enough of fighting other people's dirty little wars, clearing up the mess made by stupid politicians. And it was more than burn-out: it was the constant fear and self-loathing.

Brake lights on the Mercedes flared, it slowed, then turned right into a quiet residential street where big old detached houses faced one another across a narrow island of mature trees.

Samantha followed, moving at little more than walking pace, then parked away from the glow of street lamps, under the spreading branches of chestnut trees heavy with summer foliage. The black car had pulled up outside a house about half way down the street. The swarthy little man emerged, strutted down a short garden path, climbed stone steps to a massive front door, and let himself in. Minutes later he emerged with three women. He appeared to be haranguing them, gesturing angrily towards the distant end of the street. Two of the women headed off. The third, a woman with stylishly cut hair that had been dyed a vivid red, climbed into the Mercedes beside him.

When the two women reached the junction with the main Leeds-Barfield road, the black car pulled away from the kerb and followed, crossed straight over at the intersection and headed up a long rise that led to the moors.

Samantha slowed at the road crossing. The two women were clearly prostitutes, chased out of the house by their pimp to waylay punters returning from pubs and clubs. One stooped, peered through the windows of the Ferrari, then stepped back, no longer interested when she saw the driver was a woman.

Back home, Samantha went through the habitual security routine, then closed the garage doors and climbed up to the second floor. She undressed, showered, then descended to the sitting room and poured herself a large whisky. Pulling her lap-top from beneath a pile of fashion magazines at the end of the sofa, she powered it up and loaded the disk Marcus had given her; began to scroll through the data and images, noting material relevant to the Leeds-Sheffield-Bradford triangle.

The red-haired woman she'd seen climbing into the Mercedes an hour earlier was the wife of Enver Vrakimi, an Albanian into prostitution and credit card scams. The car's swarthy little driver was listed as an associate. Intelligence and surveillance had worked hard: the images were vividly clear, the information comprehensive. She committed names, addresses, faces, to memory; copied telephone numbers into a small pocket book. The pieces of the jigsaw were slipping into place. It was all as she'd suspected.

*   *   *

Betty Slater let herself into the conservatory, then unlocked the back door and stepped into the kitchen.

'Jack?'

There was no answering voice. Betty listened to the silence of the house for a few thudding heartbeats, then looked around. Dirty dishes were stacked in the sink; the remains of a meal were strewn across the table. Suddenly remembering, she glanced back into the conservatory. The pile of blood-soaked clothes had gone.

Betty made for the hall, climbed the stairs and entered the tiny front bedroom. The doors of the bulkhead cupboard were still hanging open, but all traces of her embarrassing loss of bladder control had evaporated away. She picked up a suitcase, carried it through to the bedroom she shared with Jack, and threw it down on the bed. She began to fill it with her decent underwear and best clothes, her small tapered fingers deftly smoothing fabric, packing garments carefully in spite of a craving to be out of the house.

She'd phoned repeatedly the previous day and through the early hours of that morning, but no one had answered. Jack could be on his way home from the factory. He could walk in at any time. Fear stabbed her, and she began to just cram things into the case.

The night and day she'd spent with Adam had been pleasant. She'd forgotten her fears and Adam seemed to have shaken off his sadness. Guilt had made him very inhibited that first night, but the following afternoon he'd shut the shop, taken her by the hand, led her up to that big canopied bed and become quite passionate in a genteel sort of way. It wasn't like being with Jack. Adam wasn't forceful; he didn't dominate her. He was tender, a little unsure of himself. Perhaps he was worried about embarrassing her. A lover could be over sensitive.

Maybe Adam was out of practice. Heavens, if he'd been telling her the truth he was a born-again virgin. And he'd insisted she stay at the shop until she'd sorted herself out. He really was a kind and thoughtful man.

Betty felt a sudden rush of angry satisfaction. She'd done it; done the thing she'd subconsciously hoped to do when she'd first realized Adam was attracted to her; done the very thing that would hurt Jack most. The thought of another man making love to her would crucify him, tear him apart, torture him for the rest of his life. She was glad: glad she'd hurt him in the only way a woman could. And Adam would care for her and watch over her now they were sleeping together.

She heard a movement downstairs. Her body stiffened and her heart began to pound.

Someone knocked on the kitchen door and a voice called up, 'Anyone home? Mrs Slater? Anyone home?'

Betty returned to the stairs and descended to the first landing. She could see them now, in the hall, staring up at her, a policeman and a policewoman, scrubbed clean and looking smart in their uniforms. A hissing radio was clicking on and off, emitting staccato bursts of garbled speech.

'Mrs Slater?' the policewoman asked.

'That's right.'

'I think you should come and sit down. I'm afraid we've some rather distressing news for you.'

'News?'

The policewoman climbed the stairs to the landing, took her by the arm, led her into the sitting room and gently eased her on to the sofa.

The policeman removed his cap. 'I'm sorry, Mrs Slater, but your husband's had an accident.'

'Accident? Is it serious?'

'I'm afraid he's dead, Mrs Slater. I'm very sorry.'

The policewoman sat down beside her. Betty felt her arm sliding around her shoulders.

'How . . . ?'

'It happened at the factory,' the policeman said. 'The foreman called us when he arrived for work this morning. It looks as if your husband fell into a big concrete mixer when it was turning and he couldn't climb out.'

'Can I see him?' The accident hadn't revived her affection for Jack. She wanted to make sure he was dead.

Betty felt the policewoman's arm tighten around her shoulders and a cool little hand take hold of hers.

'We wouldn't advise you to, Mrs Slater,' the policeman said. 'He'd been tumbling around in the drum for several hours before he was found. You wouldn't be able to recognize him.' The policeman swallowed hard. The tangled mess of rags and bloody flesh hadn't seemed remotely human when he'd shone his lamp on it.

'Really!' Betty gasped. She was numb with shock. Not as someone newly bereaved, more like a prisoner unexpectedly released.

'Would you like me to make you a cup of tea?' the policewoman asked.

'Tea? I . . . Er, no thanks,' Betty mumbled.

'Did your husband have a dentist?' the policeman asked. Betty nodded. 'Drew and James. The surgery's on Ropergate.'

The policeman noted it down.

'Why do you want to know?'

'We may need dental records to identify the body. We'll have to investigate the death and there'll be an inquest. Did your husband have a hairbrush or a comb?'

'It's upstairs, in the bathroom. Why do you . . . ?'

'The coroner may ask for a corroborating tissue match. The forensic people could use hairs from a comb.'

'Is the body that bad, then?' Betty asked.

'I'm afraid so, Mrs Slater. Would you allow me to have the comb?' The policeman began to take deep breaths, trying to hold back an urge to vomit. A night-long tumbling in the drum, repeated dropping on to those big metal paddles, had hacked the body into its component parts.

'It's upstairs. I'll get it for you,' Betty

mumbled, and rose to her feet.

'Would you like me to come?' the policewoman asked.

'No, love. It's OK.'

When she returned around the landing with the brush and comb the policewoman was gazing anxiously up the stairs. Betty descended and handed them over. The policewoman held them delicately between finger and thumb, her male colleague opened a plastic bag, and she dropped them inside.

'Do you have any family we could contact for you?' the policewoman asked.

Betty shook her head.

'Any friends or neighbours?'

Betty's face brightened a little. 'Yes, I've got a friend. I'll go and . . .'

'Perhaps we could drive you there?' the policeman said.

'It's not far. Just over the street and down the hill towards town. I'll go when I've got my breath back. But thanks, anyway.'

'Sure you'll be OK?' the policeman asked.

Betty nodded, followed them through the kitchen and into the conservatory. 'What about the factory and the men?' she asked, as an afterthought.

'We've had to close it down until the forensic people have gone over it. We'll be in touch about that. We've taken the keys.'

Joyful thoughts flooded Betty's mind. There was Jack's life insurance, the mortgage would be paid off, and the business had been doing so well he'd almost worn his boots out traipsing to the bank to make deposits. She was rich and free. Her gran had been right: one of God's angels had been watching over her.

CHAPTER FOURTEEN

Samantha cruised slowly down the Leeds-Barfield road, looking for the street of big old detached houses she'd driven along the previous night. It was a little after five, and the convoy of homebound workers would probably bring the prostitutes to the road junction.

Two micro-skirted young women were there. She could see them up ahead, one in high heels, the other in thigh-high boots. They looked drab, almost unkempt, as they tried to make eye contact with potential punters in the slowly moving line of cars.

Samantha turned out of the convoy and into the quiet sleepy street where high windows were keeping secrets and summer foliage was heavy on mature trees. She drove past the house, found a vacant space, and parked the Ferrari.

Carrying her attaché case, she made her way back and climbed stone steps to the shade of the porch. She rang the bell, then tapped on

216

the frosted glass panel of the big entrance door.

No one answered. Perhaps they were all out plying their trade. Samantha knocked and rang again, then turned the battered brass knob. The door opened when she pushed, and she stepped into a wide hallway. High ceilings, pale blue flock wallpaper, a deep blue carpet with a floral pattern: the decorations were tired, faded and tasteless.

Samantha glanced towards the stairs. Standing with her hand on top of a carved oak newel post was the woman with the bright red hair. Behind her stood a girl, not much more than a child, dressed in jeans and a skimpy T-shirt.

'Mrs Vrakimi?'

The woman's eyes widened with surprise. She turned and whispered something, then the girl moved around her, ran down the hall and disappeared through a door that opened into a room at the back of the house.

Samantha approached the foot of the stairs and looked up at her. She was slim and fairly tall. Her breasts were impressive, but narrow hips robbed the rest of her body of shape, made it seem almost boyish. Her faded print dress buttoned up the front, her white high-heeled shoes were scuffed and cheap looking. She wasn't wearing tights or stockings.

'I'd like to talk to you if I may, Mrs Vrakimi.' Samantha spoke the words in

Albanian, keeping her voice low. She flicked open her Serious Crimes Unit wallet and allowed the woman a fleeting glance.

'Who are you, and what do you want with me?' The woman began to fiddle with one of the buttons on her dress while her eyes ranged nervously over Samantha's face. Samantha could feel her fear.

'Albanian Ministry of the Interior,' Samantha murmured glibly. 'I need to talk to you for a few moments. Is there somewhere private we . . .'

'If you're from Immigration, my husband has my passport and papers. You must speak to him. He's not here now.'

'I'm not from Immigration,' Samantha said gently. 'I'm here to help you, but first we have to talk.'

'No!' the woman protested. 'You want to get me killed?' Anger was surfacing through her fear now.

'If you do nothing you'll be killed sooner or later,' Samantha said. 'You know that, don't you? Killed like the other women and children Vakrimi's spirited away.'

'You don't understand what you could be doing to me. You must leave.'

'Don't you want to do something for the child?' Samantha nodded towards the door at the end of the hall. 'Does she enjoy having sex with old men?'

'I've no idea what you're talking about. You

218

must go . . .'

The door at the end of the hall opened and a black haired woman, her poor complexion redeemed by huge dark eyes, peered at them.

'You OK, Maria?'

'Fine,' Maria Vrakimi said. 'It's just some lezzie business woman looking for someone to go down on her.'

Samantha smiled. The two women were conversing in Polish, unaware that she could understand.

The dark-eyed woman looked her over. Her expression betrayed a mild curiosity, but there was no trace of surprise or contempt. The woman shrugged and said, 'Her money will smell just as sweet as a man's,' then withdrew her head and closed the door.

Maria Vrakimi beckoned Samantha to follow her. They climbed the wide creaking stairs and entered a bedroom that overlooked an untidy garden where the young girl was sitting, motionless, on a swing.

A big Edwardian headboard, with woven cane panels, rose above the double bed. Wardrobe, bedside cabinets and dressing table had been taken from different suites of furniture. The pink striped wallpaper was cheap but clean, the blue carpet unworn. In a smaller room the effect would have been homely. In that big high space it looked tacky and sparse.

Maria switched on a tiny radio, kicked off

her shoes, and began to unbutton her dress. She nodded towards the bed. 'Remove the jacket of your suit and get under the sheets.' She kept her voice below the level of the music.

Samantha did as she was asked. Then Maria, naked apart from a pair of androgynous looking cotton pants, slid into the bed and straddled her, supporting her weight on her knees and elbows, the huge brown nipples of her pendulous breasts almost brushing the lace on Samantha's slip.

'Put your arms around my neck. There are no locks on the doors and if anyone comes into the room it must look as if you're getting what you're paying for.'

Samantha slid her hands beneath the curtain of red hair and asked, 'Where is your husband?'

'Husband?' There was a sneer in Maria's voice. 'The man who has a piece of paper to say he is my husband does not come here. He lives in a big house called Moorside, above the town. Sometimes he sends Ramiz to collect me. He spends an hour humiliating and degrading me, then Ramiz brings me back. Why do you want to know?' Her lips were trembling and her eyes were bright with unshed tears.

'Because of all the women and children who are disappearing. Because of other trouble he's causing.'

'Enver would kill me if he knew I was talking to you. You don't understand how it is. He has our papers, our passports. We are here illegally and have no money and little English. Ramiz is always watching us. No one dare complain. Anyone who becomes difficult is beaten or raped or killed.'

'Would you like to be Vrakimi's widow?'

'And what would become of me then? Prison? Deported back to Albania? Taken over by a man worse than Enver?'

'I would make sure you were protected, taken to a safe place, given asylum.'

Maria grunted, spread her legs and allowed the lower half of her body to rest on Samantha's thighs. 'I'm sorry, I couldn't go on holding myself up like that.' She wriggled and slid her arms beneath the pillow. 'And what would you want from me?' she asked, when she was more comfortable.

'Cooperation in catching and punishing men who've accepted bribes from your husband; men who've been making it possible for him to operate.' Samantha tried to shift her hips. 'Must we lie like this?'

'If you want to talk, we lie like this. Liliana could become curious and come in.'

'Think about the future,' Samantha said. 'If you do nothing what will happen to you and the child in the yard? You're no more than commodities Vrakimi will sooner or later replace.'

'I don't think about the future. Tomorrow, next week, next month: for me time is not measured in hours but in men I have to please.'

'Don't you think about the child I saw you with, and all the other children Vrakimi exploits?'

Maria averted her gaze, then whispered bitterly, 'You do not know the things I have endured, the things I have seen. How dare you ask me what I think about?'

Samantha cupped Maria's cheek in the palm of her hand and turned her head, forcing her look at her. Transfixing her with the green blaze of her eyes, she said softly, 'I can set you free. I can set all of you free.'

Maria laughed. 'Enver has three prostitute houses in Barfield; many houses in Leeds and Bradford and other places whose names I do not know. How can you set all the women free?'

'When Vrakimi and all his helpers are gone, they will be free.'

'You will chase them away?' Maria sneered.

'I will kill them. They will all be dead. You will be the widow of Vrakimi.'

Maria propped herself up on her hands so she could study Samantha's face. After a while, she said, 'You'd better tell me what you want to know; what part I will have to play in all of this.'

Samantha rolled Maria on to her back,

reached down the side of the bed and picked up her case. She clicked it open, took out a swatch of glossy photographs she'd purchased from the *Barfield Gazette* and some pictures she'd torn from the society pages of the county magazines.

Maria gestured for her to put the case back on the floor and whispered, 'Climb on to me. Liliana might come in and I don't trust her. If she sees anything strange she'll tell Ramiz and he'll tell Enver and then God knows what will happen.'

Samantha hitched her tight skirt up around her waist, sat astride Maria and began to show her group photographs of the local great and good: hunt balls, charity dinners, fund-raising parties. 'Do you recognize any of these men? Do they come here? Do any of them use the young girls?'

Maria squinted, trying to focus on images that were too close to her face. Presently she said, 'Him', and turned the photograph so Samantha could see. 'He's the local police chief. He comes here every Tuesday night, always about eleven, wearing a dinner jacket and black bow tie. He carries a case like yours.'

'And?'

Maria shrugged. 'He keeps a big medallion in the case. It's on a broad ribbon of many colours.' She moved her hands from her shoulders to beneath her breasts. 'It would hang about here. I see it when he takes his

223

watch and cuff-links off because he always opens the case and drops them inside. He never pays. It's a favour from Enver. We never have trouble from the police.'

'He's probably on his way home from the lodge when he stops off here,' Samantha said.

'They have hunting lodges in England?'

Samantha smiled. 'It's a sort of boys' club: a secret society. Members of the police seem attracted to it. Does he ever say anything?'

Maria shrugged. 'No. He just tells me what he wants me to do, like commands. He's cold, arrogant. I hate him.'

Samantha shuffled the photographs. Maria had got the man's title wrong. He was Barfield's deputy chief constable, not the chief constable.

'Does Vrakimi arrange favours for anyone else?'

'Friday evenings. A car collects about a dozen women from his places in Barfield and Leeds and takes them to a party at the big house.'

'Moorside?'

Maria nodded. 'Three or four young girls are taken, too.'

'How young?'

'Mostly between twelve and fourteen, but I've seen younger girls. Enver provides decent clothes for us and we change when we get to the house. The young ones are dressed as schoolgirls, or they wear white confirmation dresses or party frocks. Sometimes the older women are told to plait their hair.'

'Who attends these parties?'

Maria beckoned for the photographs and magazine clippings. Samantha held them under the sheet for her, one by one, while Maria said, 'Him, and him, and him,' until she'd pointed out six or seven men.

'Which ones like young girls?'

'These two.' Maria pointed to one of the glossy photographs. 'There are more, but their pictures are not here.'

'The girls; they'd recognize the men?' Samantha asked.

'How could they forget? They'll take the memory of their faces and what they do to them to the grave.'

'So,' Samantha murmured thoughtfully. 'The police chief will be seeing you tomorrow night.'

'Tomorrow?'

'Tuesday: tomorrow is Tuesday, the day the police chief calls.'

Maria shrugged. 'I lose track of the days. Sure, tomorrow.'

'And the big party will be at Moorside on Friday?'

'Not this week. It's being held on Wednesday instead. On Friday Zoran Karlensa meets Enver at Moorside to talk business. I overheard Ramiz phoning everyone, arranging women for Wednesday and for Enver's minders to be there on Friday. Karlensa supplies passports and travel papers for Enver's girls.'

'Will you be at Moorside on Wednesday?' Samantha asked.

Maria nodded. 'It pleases some of the men to think they've had sex with their host's wife.'

Samantha reached over the side of the bed and took a small nylon make-up bag from her case. 'This has a camera inside,' she said. 'Could you put it on the dressing table when the police chief is here?'

'He'll hear it running.'

'There are no moving parts; it's silent.' Samantha shuffled up the bed until Maria's breasts nestled between her thighs. She unzipped the case and showed Maria the empty interior. 'Look, there's nothing to see. You could fill it with cosmetics if you want. The camera's in the lining. You just point the end with the black beads towards the thing you want to film, then unzip it to set it going.'

Maria gazed at the nylon bag for a few moments, then shrugged and said, 'What the hell, I suppose I could do that. I loathe the bastard.'

'Could you take it to Moorside, put it in the room where the men have sex with the young girls?'

Maria became fearful. 'I take nothing.'

'Put make-up in it.'

'All that we need is there: clothes, make-up.

Enver provides it so we look smart and sexy for his friends. I daren't take a thing like that to Moorside. Vrakimi, Ramiz, one of his other men, could take it from me. They'd kill me if they found out what it was. And anyway, young girls are in more than one room.'

Samantha gazed down at Maria. Vrakimi's guests were invited because they held positions of power and influence. She had to have strong evidence or smart lawyers would ensure they never faced trial.

'Presumably they use condoms?' Samantha said.

'Always. They're heaped in bowls on the bedside tables.'

'And afterwards?'

'Afterwards?'

'What do they do with them?'

'Drop them in plastic buckets beside the bed.'

'And then what?'

'One of us has to go round the rooms, collect the buckets and take them down to the basement. There are anthracite furnaces there: one for heating, one for hot water. Winter, summer, there is always one burning; the rubbers are thrown into the fire. And there are big stone sinks down there for rinsing out the buckets. Vrakimi insists that the rubbers are burnt, never flushed down the toilets.'

'Could you collect them and leave the buckets in the basement?'

Maria wrinkled her nose. 'What would you want buckets of used contraceptives for?'

'DNA sampling. If you can't film the men, a test on the semen would at least prove they were there. If the buckets from the young girls' rooms were marked, it would identify the men who'd abused them.'

'And how would you get the buckets?'

'That's something I'll have to work on.'

Maria sighed. 'OK, I do it for you. But only two buckets, one for women, one for girls. There could be maybe ten, twelve, buckets in use. I couldn't hide so many.'

'Where will you put them?'

'There's a wine cellar across from the boiler room. It's not used. I'll put the buckets in there, under one of the stone shelves.'

Samantha gathered the photographs and cuttings together, climbed off Maria and rose from the bed. She tugged her skirt down and reached for her jacket. Maria followed, pulling on her dress and buttoning it up.

'I must have the camera when you've used it tomorrow night,' Samantha said. She dropped the photographs into her case and clicked it shut.

'He usually leaves around midnight. Watch the house from under the trees. I'll throw it into the front yard.'

Samantha reached for her bag. 'How much?'

'How much?' Maria was preoccupied,

obviously fearful of having committed herself and perhaps regretting it already.

'For our little roll on the bed?'

Maria glanced at her watch. They'd been about half an hour. 'A hundred,' she said absently. 'Anything less and they'd suspect something.'

*   *   *

Samantha viewed the pale-blue Moschino suit with distaste. Its jacket was pristine, but the skirt was crumpled after being yanked up around her waist. Sod it! Her Majesty's Government would have to foot the dry cleaning bill. She'd head the claim 'Brothel Expenses'; that should give Marcus a laugh.

She put it on a hanger, went down to the sitting room, poured a drink and switched on the television. Armed police, emergency services, smoke-filled gloom and wreckage filled the screen. Suicide bombers had hit the underground again. She clicked through the channels. Two explosions in stations, five on trains moving through the tunnels. Concerned presenters were jabbering away, spreading the news, their urgent voices over the flickering pictures conveying a sense of apocalyptic dread.

Samantha drained her glass and poured another drink. Intelligence people, from the chief to way below Marcus, would be getting a ministerial battering tonight. Allowing the first attack to happen would have been considered a serious lapse. Another seven strikes not many more days later would be regarded as sheer incompetence.

She ought to turn her attention to the terrorists, show some results to justify the pay. But she was nearing closure on the Vrakimi business, and the main players were all included on the disk Marcus had given her. She'd spend a couple more days on it. That would give her time to get an all-over air brush tan and buy a jilbab and hijab, maybe a thobe, too: some more items Her Majesty's Government would be footing the bill for. She'd head that item 'Protective Clothing'. It wouldn't be wise to let Marcus or anyone else know too much about her methods.

Samantha powered up her laptop, began to search for data on Zoran Karlensa, the man Maria had said her husband was meeting on Friday. It was all there, a model of brevity: names, phone numbers, places, dates, rackets.

She connected an unallocated phone to the laptop and entered a series of digits, turning it into a clone of Ramiz Manos's mobile. She keyed Karlensa's ex-directory number into the clone, then sat back and watched the mayhem on television while she listened to the purr of the dialing tone. She was about to ring off when the line clicked.

'Hullo?'

'Karlensa? Zoran Karlensa?'

'Who is this?' The guttural voice was angry. 'How did you get this number?'

'I'm an enemy of Vrakimi. I got your number from his papers.'

'No one has this number. You couldn't have got . . .'

'Are we going to waste time talking about stupid numbers, or are you going to listen to what I have to say?'

'Who is this?' The voice was really angry now. He was used to respect.

'You're meeting Vrakimi on Friday, at Moorside. You think you're having a business meeting to discuss mutual concerns, supplying him with papers and passports, stuff like that.'

'How do you know this?'

'I overhear Vrakimi talking. I hear him saying things you ought to know.'

'Things? What things?'

'He wants your passport business. He knows you run it from Leeds: that house in Flowitt Street. He resents the way it gives you a hold over him, resents having to pay for papers for his women. And he's been checking out your other interests.'

Samantha let it rest there, remained silent, listened to the hiss on the line and the sound of Karlensa's laboured breathing.

Presently she heard a cough, and the throaty voice said, 'What other interests?'

'The credit card scam you run from

Bradford; all the club bouncers you have on the payroll so you can get your pushers in. He's got a list of names.'

'Who the hell are you?'

'Someone who hates and fears Vrakimi as much as you should; someone who watches and listens.'

Asthmatic wheezing panted down the line, but Karlensa didn't speak.

Presently she said, 'He's moving men in for the Friday meeting. They're going to gun you down so he can take over. And that woman you're with at the moment, the beautiful Romanian blonde, Elena, I heard them laughing about putting her in one of the brothels. And you know what they do to make new women compliant, don't you, Karlensa? Maybe you've been to some of those parties: bring a bottle and line up to rape the girl?'

The wheezing became more laboured. 'Why should you tell me all this? I think you're just some lying whore winding me up so I'll settle scores for you.'

'Do you think Vrakimi's stupid whores would know the things I've told you? Would they know you started moving cocaine into Dublin a month ago? I know because I've listened to Vrakimi talking to little Ramiz Manos and the others. Vrakimi knows because after Friday he's taking over.'

There was more wheezing and coughing at the other end of the line. The conversation hadn't done anything for Zoran Karlensa's asthma. Samantha heard a gasping intake of breath, sensed he was going to speak, and switched off the cloned mobile.

She tossed it down on the sofa, then leafed through the papers in her case until she found the emergency powers booklet Marcus had given her. She checked the number of the armourer he'd written inside the back cover, lifted her encrypted phone from the case, and dialed it. Almost instantly, a breezy male voice said, 'Stationery and Office Equipment.'

'Ulrich?'

'I'll put you through.'

The line clicked and a woman's voice said, 'Ulrich speaking.'

'I understand you're the armourer.'

'Armourer? What's an armourer? This is Stationery and Office Equipment. Give me the second and sixth digits of your first security code.'

Samantha recited the numbers.

'Now the first and third of your second code.'

Samantha obliged. She could hear a keyboard clicking.

'What's your password?'

'Bethsheba.'

'I'm the armourer, Bethsheba. What do you want?'

'Something to take out two, no, make that three, cars. Nothing too noisy, but it's got to be effective.'

'You want some Holy Ghosts.'

'Holy Ghosts?'

'That's what we call these packages. Incendiary devices. Intense heat, melt the inside of a tank, but no explosion. Only noise comes from the expanding air. Blinding light, roaring wind: Holy Ghost.'

'Sounds good,' Samantha said.

'Timer or remote?'

'Mmm, better make them remote. And simultaneously activated.'

'Anything else?'

'A decent sub.'

'How about a Heckler MP5?'

'A Heckler and Koch will do nicely,' Samantha said.

'Silenced?'

'May as well. I think that's it.'

'I'll have them couriered to you. When and where?'

'Tomorrow morning. Barfield railway station. I'll be sitting on one of the benches outside the ticket hall at ten.'

'The delivery man will be in black motorcycle leathers and a black helmet. Just say, "Are you Mr Shitsu?".'

Samantha began to laugh. 'Mr Shitsu? Who dreamt that one up?'

'I did. And don't laugh when you ask him. He's six-six and sensitive. He'll ask you for the first and last digits of your second security code. Have them ready or he'll just walk away. He'll also ask you to sign and print a name on a delivery docket. What's it going to be?'

'Shirley Temple.'

'Shirley and Shitsu: doesn't have quite the same ring as Bonny and Clyde.' Ulrich was laughing now.

'I don't intend to rob any banks.' Sensing the woman was going to ring off, Samantha said, 'Ulrich?'

'Yeah?'

'Better include a few hundred rounds for the sub and a couple of boxes of shells for a nine-millimetre automatic.'

'Will do,' Ulrich said. 'And one last thing: look away when you detonate the packages. The glare can burn your retinas off.'

'Thanks,' Samantha said. 'Thanks a lot.'

CHAPTER FIFTEEN

Samantha tugged at the strap of her shoulder holster; eased the gun butt down and forward a little to stop it pressing into the side of her breast. She'd been lying amongst the gorse for almost an hour now. Zoran Karlensa was probably waiting until nightfall; either that or her baiting hadn't roused him and he'd decided not to keep his appointment with Enver Vrakimi.

235

Dormer windows, peering out of Moorside's blue-slate roof, were reflecting the last of the setting sun. Lower down the stone façade, a dozen unlit windows made rectangles of darkness.

Lifting the binoculars, she studied the front of the house and what she could see of the grounds. Detail was blurring in the fading light, but she could still make out the long gravel drive, the ornate iron gates that had been pegged open, and high garden walls, leaning a little here and there, and covered with ivy where they ran down the side of the house. Doric columns supported a flat stone canopy over panelled entrance doors, one of which was opening. It was the first sign of life.

Samantha sharpened the focus on the binoculars. When the man in the porch turned and pulled open the other door she could see it was Ramiz Manos, Vrakimi's little minder.

A pair of German shepherd dogs bounded past him and began to frisk around on the half-acre parking area. Manos waved his arms and yelled at the dogs, calling them back into the house, but the sound didn't carry over the distance. Eventually the dogs obeyed, and Manos followed them, closing an inner glazed door behind him. A light came on in the hall and formed a solitary speck of brightness on the shadowy façade.

Things were starting to happen. Within minutes, a red Volvo estate car and a big black

Audi had turned off the road and swept up to the parking area. Nine men climbed out and strode towards the porticoed entrance.

Samantha rose from the bushes and began to run over tussocky grass, down the steeply sloping moor. Crossing the road, she crept along the side of the high stone wall that flanked the garden, found a spot where the mortar had decayed, then clambered up and sat astride ivy-covered coping stones.

From her vantage, she had a view over an unkempt shrubbery towards the parking area in front of the house. They'd left a minder behind the wheel of the Volvo estate: she could see his white collar and cuffs, the gleam of a shaved head. Rolling off the top of the wall, she dropped down behind the bushes and began to move towards the cars.

Samantha unfastened the strap securing the automatic in its holster, slid back the safety catch and wrapped her hand around the grip. The man keeping watch over the transport had to be disposed of. She drew the pistol, groped in the pocket of her anorak for the silencer, and screwed it on to the muzzle as she moved through the bushes.

Close now, she could see the man drumming his fingers on the steering wheel. He suddenly turned and looked towards her. Samantha jerked down, heard the car door groan open, the crunch of feet stepping on to gravel. Tightening her grip on the gun, she waited for him to appear.

She heard the patter of liquid on leaves, then sank on to her knee so she could peer through a gap in the foliage. Legs spread wide, he was holding a circumcised penis rather delicately between finger and thumb, waving it from side to side, playfully scattering the copious golden stream.

Slowly, soundlessly, Samantha brought up the gun and shot him in the left eye. His head jerked back, his knees sagged, and he collapsed towards her into the rhododendron bush.

Samantha rose to her feet and rounded the bush. His legs were sticking out across the gravel. Thankful she was wearing surgical gloves, she reached down, grabbed his ankles and tugged at the body until it was hidden beneath the urine splattered foliage. She made a mental note to dump the anorak.

Sounds of raised voices and barking dogs escaped from the house, then, riding over it all, the staccato clatter of a sub-machine gun. Barking turned into a frenzied howling, and shouts were drowned by shotgun blasts.

Taking Ulrich's Holy Ghosts from the folds of her anorak, she peeled off crimson patches and tugged at exposed priming rings, activating the devices. She crossed over to the open door of the Volvo estate, slid a package under the driver's seat, then crunched over the gravel and planted the other two beneath the front seat of the big Audi.

The house was completely silent now. Samantha returned to the high garden wall, took the detonator from the pocket of her anorak, and keyed in the activating sequence. She waited.

Men burst from the house, ran across the gravel and began to climb into the cars. There was an argument about the missing minder, then someone slid behind the wheel of the Volvo and starters whined. A straggler appeared in the porch, clutching a briefcase, dashed after the Audi, and squeezed inside.

Samantha turned to face the wall and pressed the red firing key. Blinding light cast hard black shadows of leaves and branches against the mellowed stone wall. There was a rumble, like distant thunder, and a rushing wind tore at the foliage.

She waited until the reflected glare had dimmed, then turned. Haloes of flame surrounded twin balls of blinding light. The house was on the edge of the moors, high above the town, and the conflagration would be seen from highways and byways all over Barfield. There wasn't much time. Pistol in hand, she dashed through the bushes and entered the house.

A body lay, face down, on the stairs, dusted over with plaster dislodged from the wall by a shotgun blast. She went through all the ground floor rooms: two big salons at the front, a kitchen and two others at the rear. Everything was opulent and tastefully expensive.

She climbed wide red-carpeted stairs, stepped over three more bodies on the landing and headed down a central corridor. Passing through a doorway, she found herself in a brightly-lit room where a lavish buffet had been laid out on a long table. She recognized some of the death-slackened faces from the images on the disk Marcus had given her. Enver Vrakimi was lying half under the table, the white linen cloth brushing his chest. Ramiz Manos, his little minder, had slumped into the food and his blood had oozed amongst piles of starched napkins and silver cutlery.

There was so little time. Samantha could do no more than count the dead before making a quick tour of bedrooms where Vrakimi's women and girls gratified the desires of men he wanted to manipulate and control. Tonight the only occupiers were a pair of German shepherd dogs and a black man with a shaved head and an expensive suit. They were all dead.

A muffled explosion rattled windows and made doors slam. Samantha tugged aside heavy drapes and looked down at the blaze in front of the house. A ball of flame was rising from the most distant car. Its petrol tank had ruptured.

She climbed a narrow flight of stairs that rose off the end of the corridor and led to what had been servants' quarters on the floor above. They weren't servants' quarters now: Vrakimi had carried out a lavish refurbishment. This was his hideaway, his own private space, isolated from the rooms he used for impressing, entertaining, rendering favours.

Samantha peered into a couple of bedrooms, a bathroom, and a sitting room, all decorated and furnished in a simple but expensive way. Opening the last door, she found herself in an office lined with monitors that were relaying views of the grounds and the rooms she'd passed through. Dated video cassettes were neatly arranged on shelves that ran the length of one wall.

Time was passing. She darted back to the bedroom, tugged black silk covers from a couple of pillows, returned to the office and filled them with videos from the shelves. Ejecting tapes from the three recording machines, she dropped them in a sack with the rest.

Apart from some computer disks, the desk drawers held nothing of interest. Cash, passports, valuables, would be locked away in a safe somewhere. She dropped the disks into a sack, grabbed a laptop from the desk and took a last look around the office. Through its tall window, set high in the gable wall, she could see Barfield, glittering in the valley below; and, at a distance, a chain of flashing lights snaking its way up to the moors and the house.

Samantha had hoped to check the basement, make sure that Maria had kept her promise and hidden the buckets of used condoms, but there was no more time. Clutching the makeshift sacks and laptop, she dashed down two flights of stairs and ran from the house. She kept within the bushes while she skirted the burning wreckage on the driveway, crouched low when she slipped out of the gates, not wanting to form a moving silhouette against the still brilliant light.

Turning down the side of the walled garden, she began to descend the steep gorse-covered slope at the rear of the house. Half-running, half-slithering, dragging the sacks of video tapes behind her, she was breathless when she reached the lower twist of the road a hundred feet below.

The Ferrari was just as she'd left it, hidden in the derelict cattle shed. Dropping sacks and laptop behind the seats, she climbed inside, then slid the safety catch over on the pistol and secured it in its holster. She keyed the starter, lurched out on to the road, and began to meander back to Barfield along lanes that wound through tiny villages.

Pulling into a pub yard, Samantha used a public phone to make an anonymous call to Barfield CID. After getting an assurance from the female detective chief inspector that Vrakimi's women and girls would be taken to a safe house, she supplied the names of likely paedophiles, amused at the woman's incredulity when she told her there were semen samples and where they were hidden. She didn't place any great value on the promise of a safe house. She didn't mention the deputy chief constable's weekly sex sessions, either. That was a bargaining counter she was saving for later.

*   *   *

Samantha tossed her Janet Reger slip on to the bed and pushed down the matching blue silk knickers. A surprised-looking dusky-brown stranger stared back at her from the mirror. The woman at the salon had been an artist with the air-brush; the dark skin tone was perfectly even, and the effect at the hair line and around her eyes reassuringly natural.

She'd told her it would take a day and a night for the pigment to be properly absorbed into her skin. Samantha pulled on a bathrobe. She'd spend the time catching up on phone calls and preparing a report for Marcus. And there were those videos from Moorside to wade through.

Groping under the pile of fashion magazines on the sofa, she found the clone of Ramiz Manos's mobile between the cushions, and dialed Barfield CID. She asked for James Conrad, the deputy chief constable.

'I'm afraid Mr Conrad's in a meeting and he's not taking calls,' said a cool female voice.

'Tell him I have information about Maria Vrakimi. Tell him if he's too busy to talk right now, I'll leave the message with Mrs Conrad.'

After a few seconds the line clicked and a belligerent voice with a pronounced Yorkshire accent demanded, 'Who's speaking? Who wants to talk to me about Mrs Vrakimi?'

Samantha sensed he'd be quick to ring off. Trying to make sure he stayed on the line, she said softly, 'Does your wife know you've been screwing Maria Vrakimi every Tuesday night for God knows how long? You stop off for your little sex sessions on your way home from the lodge, don't you?'

'I . . . Who is this?'

'Just answer the question.'

'This is ridiculous,' the voice blustered. 'Why should I answer your stupid questions. There's nothing for my wife to know.'

'You're telling porkies, James.' Samantha's tone was mocking. 'I've got a crystal clear DVD of you giving Maria what the boys on the force call a right seeing to. I'm watching it now. Maria's on her knees, holding on to that big old headboard with the woven cane panels, and you've left your little attaché case open. I can see all your regalia.'

'Who the bloody hell are you?' Conrad snarled.

'I'll send you a copy,' Samantha said.

244

'Meanwhile, there's something you've got to organize today or your wife gets the disk, gift wrapped, special delivery, tomorrow.'

'This is outrageous. You can't treat . . .'

'James,' Samantha interrupted reprovingly. 'If you want to keep your job and avoid a messy divorce you'd better keep quiet and listen to me, OK?'

She listened to the silence on the line for a moment, then went on, 'There's a construction site in the borough, some Ethnic Minorities Welfare Centre. They've used big concrete blocks to build a retaining wall. You've got to arrange for a hole to be cut into block one-three-six: the numbers are scratched into the groove along the bottom edge. Have the hole cut about half-a-metre in from the left-hand end and a metre and a half up from the base. Make it the size of a dinner plate. The borough engineer will know how to form the hole, but you've got to make sure it's done today.'

'You're crazy! Why the hell should I arrange for some stupid hole cutting?'

'Because you want to keep your job and because you're going to find a body in the block. And when you've done that you'll have to arrange for the rest of the blocks to be opened up. There's more than one body in the wall.'

Samantha switched off the phone.

CHAPTER SIXTEEN

Samantha rolled on black nylon knee-highs, then reached for her boots. They were the only suitable footwear she had; modest Muslim women wouldn't trot to the mosque in strappy Jimmy Choos.

Sliding her arms into the sleeves of a shapeless black chiffon dress, she drew it over her head and pulled it down. The hem was regulation ankle length, but the sleeves were too long. Taking a couple of elastic hair bands, she positioned them just above her elbows, bunching the black fabric and lifting the cuffs up to her wrists. Nothing, but nothing, must hinder the movement of her hands.

The black ankle-length coat charmed her less than the dress. She slipped it on, buttoned it up to her neck and smoothed down the collar. Thobe and jilbab: she shuddered.

Samantha picked up the last package from the bed and glanced at the label. 'The Two-Piece Amira Hijab. Good for women on the go'. That was her all right, a woman on the go. With a resigned little sigh, she tore away the cellophane, took the tight-fitting woven hat, and pulled it on. She tucked her hair inside and adjusted the dove-grey material until it was half way down her brow. Unfolding the larger, shawl-like covering, she arranged it over the hat, spread its dark-grey material across her shoulders and pulled it forward to her chin.

She studied the effect in the mirror. Eyes, nose, cheeks, mouth: nothing else was exposed, not even a solitary strand of hair. She looked younger: much younger. She'd pass for eighteen, maybe less in a kind light. There was something to be said for the hijab, after all.

Searching amongst the clutter on her dressing table, she found the spectacles and slid them on. Black wire frames holding slightly tinted plain glass, they dulled the brilliance of her eyes, made her look studious and virginal. Her appearance had to be perfect. The illusion had to work first time and every time. There would be no second chances.

Descending to the kitchen, Samantha took jars of honey from a cupboard and put them in a big canvas shopping bag. She screwed the silencer on to the automatic pistol and laid it on top. After covering jars and pistol with a tea towel, she made her way down to the garage and the Ferrari.

*   *   *

Barfield's mosque was located on a grassy rise beyond the inner ring road. A large but unpretentious building of smooth red brick, its entrance and what Samantha took to be an

247

office and meeting rooms were grouped around an octagonal prayer hall.

The minaret was no more than a gesture; just a brick chimney-like structure capped by a small concrete dome that was surmounted by a bronze crescent.

Samantha descended into the gloom of the underpass, did her best to avoid the pools of stagnant water as she walked along the litter-strewn tunnel to the other side of the road.

When she emerged, she realized there was no direct pathway to the mosque. It could only be reached through an area of near derelict housing that included low- and high-rise flats. Heading down the nearest street, she came to a cleared area ringed by security fencing, where a site board announced that Bartlets of Barfield were building an Ethnic Minorities Welfare Centre for the borough.

It was the job that was causing Emma Turner so much concern; the job where they'd used the big concrete blocks. Samantha decided to make a detour. Rounding the corner of the new building, she could see that high canvas screens had been erected to hide part of a retaining wall. A black police van and a couple of police cars were parked close by. Work on the building seemed to have been suspended. The only sounds were coming from behind the screen: the whine of drilling machinery and the occasional clatter of a mechanical pick. The canvas parted and a forensics officer in white overalls carrying a small freezer case emerged and headed for the black van.

James Conrad had done as she'd asked.

Samantha headed up the incline and along a new footpath that had been formed at the top of the retaining wall. She could see the mosque again from up here, and the path she had to take between the blocks of flats became clear. She walked on.

Rusty chain-link fencing, sagging in places, enclosed the mosque. A mini-bus was pulling into a parking area at the rear and, as Samantha headed down the side of the compound, children began to tumble out and fill the yard with happy chatter.

The prayer hall windows were plain rectangles of glass set beneath Moorish arches. They'd been coated with some light-reflecting film that made it impossible to see inside. Alongside a signboard that carried the message, 'There is no god but Allah and Muhammad is the messenger of God', was a pedestrian gate.

Samantha went through, headed down a path overgrown with weeds, and pushed at the entrance doors. They were locked. Inside, a young man of about twenty, wearing a nightshirt-like kameez and white cap, was looking towards her. She pushed her face close to the glass and waved. He ambled over, unlocked the door and pulled it open.

'Peace be upon you.' Samantha spoke the words in Arabic, sensed it was a language he was not fluent in, so she continued in English, 'I wish to see Ahmed Manawi. I understand he's your imam, your preacher?'

The youth searched her face. 'The imam doesn't talk with women who come alone and we don't have a woman teacher.' He spoke with a heavy Yorkshire accent.

'My name is Laila Hassam. I am the daughter of his sister's child. He is my great uncle. I bring him a message from Fatima, my grandmother, and a gift from my mother.' She begged him with her eyes.

Fleshy lips took on a contemptuous downward turn. He studied her face again, then said curtly, 'Wait. I'll tell Imam Manawi that you are here.'

Samantha bowed her head. This was Islam she reflected. He was a man, and she was of little consequence.

Children were pouring in from the back now. The youth moved through the crush of jostling bodies and disappeared through a door.

While she waited, she looked around. Glazed doors opened into the high, carpeted prayer hall. It was deserted. Along the corridor, doors gave access to what she guessed were classrooms or meeting rooms, and perhaps a library. It was all pretty basic: bare brick walls, cheap plywood flush doors that needed varnishing, and grey floor tiles.

The youth appeared in the doorway, raised his hand and beckoned her with an imperious gesture. Head modestly bowed, she followed him into the room.

'Ahmed Manawi, my great uncle?' she asked.

The elderly, bearded man wore a jubba; a long, black, full-sleeved garment that was fastened only at the neck. It reminded Samantha of a priest's cassock. Beneath it was an ankle length white shirt. An embroidered white cap covered iron-grey hair, and sandals protected his bare feet. He gazed at her thoughtfully over tiny gold-rimmed spectacles as he said in Arabic, 'I am he. And you are my sister's grandchild?'

Samantha nodded. 'Peace be with you, Uncle,' she murmured, then glanced at the youth who was standing behind the imam.

'This is Rafic. He was working for me on the computer. Do you mind if he continues? His grasp of Arabic is limited.'

Samantha shook her head. 'Of course not.'

The old man had just sentenced his chaperone to death.

The imam half turned, muttered something Samantha couldn't hear, and the young man resumed his seat at the table, began tapping at a keyboard while he worked his way down a pile of cards.

'Does your grandmother still live in the old

consul's house in Cairo?'

Realizing he was testing her, Samantha struggled to recall the data she'd taken from Marcus's disk. 'I don't remember grandmother ever living in a consul's house. I only remember going to the flat she has now. It's on Sharia Ramses, not far from the El Hakim Mosque. Perhaps she had the house before I was born.'

'And you? Where is the house of your father?'

'We live in a street behind the Sharia Corniche, close to the El Giza Bridge. My father is the ophthalmic surgeon at the Tilul El Sira hospital.' She sensed she was feeding him information he wasn't sure of himself. His family would be large and scattered. He wouldn't remember every niece and nephew, much less their husbands and wives.

'Forgive me child, but we live in dangerous times. Could you recite the first chapter of the Koran for me?'

Samantha took a deep breath:

'In the name of God, the compassionate, the merciful. Praise be to God, the Lord of creation, Master of the day of judgement. You alone we worship, and to You alone we pray for help. Guide us in the straight path, the path of those You have favoured: not those who have incurred your displeasure, nor of those who have gone astray.'

The imam was relaxing now. With his neatly

trimmed beard, his scrupulously clean appearance, the soft voice and big brown eyes, he radiated wisdom and gentleness. He seemed the kind of man any young woman would welcome as a father. Samantha studied the face intently. She had to be sure. The eyes and nose, the shape of his mouth, matched the image on the disk. And the mole was there, low on his cheek, almost hidden by the growth of beard. It was him. She was certain of it.

He smiled. 'And perhaps I could hear the sixth and seventh verses from the second chapter?'

Samantha obliged.

His smile broadened. 'I have heard an angel singing the word of God in my own tongue. You are truly the child of my sister's child.' He spread his hands. 'You have a message for me? You bring me a gift?'

Samantha reached under the cloth and brought out the gun. 'I bring you martyrdom,' she murmured softly, and shot him through the heart.

The youth turned, slack jawed, startled by the thud of the silenced gun in the confined space. Samantha squeezed the trigger again, saw the bullet hole appear, square in the centre of the youth's forehead, at the instant the imam's body hit the floor. He slumped sideways and slid out of his chair.

She held her breath. The children were still reciting the Koran in a room along the corridor and there were no sounds of doors opening or running feet.

Samantha dragged the chair the youth had been using over to the door, wedged it under the handle, then took her first good look around the room. Shelves carried religious books with ornate bindings, and there was a low table on a square of carpet with some big cushions beside it. The computer and its keyboard were standing on a beech wood table, not a desk.

Unzipping the pocket of her jilbab, she took out a wallet of tools, selected a screwdriver, and applied it to the fixings on the computer case. She withdrew the metal cover, prized out the hard disk and dropped it in her bag.

She paused and listened. The Koran was still being recited and there were no voices in the corridor. Reassured, she replaced the cover. The more time that elapsed before they discovered the disk had gone, the better.

One by one, she took down the books and flicked through the pages before replacing them. There were no documents inside and nothing behind them on the shelves.

The cards the youth had been extracting data from had scattered over the floor. Heaving his body aside with her boot, she crouched down and gathered them up, wiped blood from some on his kameez, then slid them down beside the jars of honey in her bag.

Checking the windows, she discovered they

were sealed units that didn't open. She dragged the chair away from the door and stepped out into the corridor. The chanting of children learning the Koran was louder here. When she returned to the front entrance, she found it had been locked.

Samantha ran back and explored beyond the bend in the corridor. Through a kitchen doorway she could see two women placing paper cups in rows on trays, filling them with orange juice from a plastic jug. On the far side of the kitchen, a door opened on to the parking area at the rear. She glanced through an adjoining window. The gates to the yard had been closed and padlocked. She was trapped inside.

The women were laughing and chattering; they hadn't noticed her. Heading back to the front entrance, Samantha reached into her bag for the gun, preparing to shoot out the lock. When she passed the glazed doors of the prayer hall, she glanced through and saw a fire exit on the far side.

Her boots made no sound on the carpet as she sprinted across the hall. She pushed at the locking bar, felt it lift, and she was emerging into sunlight and the rumble of traffic on the inner ring road.

Minutes later, she was striding past the construction site. The black van had been reversed up to a parting in the canvas screen and a uniformed police officer was talking earnestly with a white-coated colleague.

One job had ended; another had begun. She had to move quickly now. It wouldn't always run this smoothly. Someone would see her, remember her, and within twenty-four hours every mosque in England would have been warned about the woman in the black Jordanian style jilbab and grey hijab.

She glanced at her watch. It was a little after ten. Two men were marked for earliest possible elimination in Bradford; a group of twelve suspects in Leeds had a lower priority. With a little luck she could deal with one or the other, then drive through the night to deliver the computer disks she'd seized to Cheltenham for scanning.

*   *   *

Emma Taylor leafed through drawings in the plan chest, searching for the drainage layout for the Ethnic Minorities Welfare Centre. Preoccupied, she was only half hearing the conversation between the two trainees standing beyond the partition. And then the odd word caught her attention and she began to listen.

'. . . Cops all over the site. Arrived first thing this morning and screened off that big retaining wall. Engineers went in with a fancy diamond tipped drill and started cutting holes. Found a bloke's body.'

'A body?'

'That's not the worst part. Some sadist had hacked his cock and balls off and stuffed them in his mouth.'

'Jesus! Do they know who the dead bloke was?'

'Site foreman recognized him. Some rep from Barfield Bricks: they supplied the facings for the job. Harry . . . no, Hugh Dixon.'

Emma peered around the screen. The trainee who'd been doing the talking blushed crimson; the other sidled off and got behind his desk.

'Sorry, Mrs Turner. I didn't realize you were there. I wouldn't have . . .'

'That's all right, Chris, I quite understand,' Emma said weakly. 'What did you say the man's name was?'

'Hugh Dixon. Youngish bloke; he's a rep for Barfield Bricks.'

'Christopher?'

'Yes, Mrs Turner?'

'Could you get me a glass of water, I feel a little faint.'

CHAPTER SEVENTEEN

'Is that you, Marcus?'

'Minister! How can I help you?'

'Tried to get the chief, but she's not

available. Where is she?'

'Briefing the PM. We're having some success.'

'At a price, Marcus. At a price.' The minister sounded scathing.

'I don't follow you, Minister.' Marcus braced himself. He knew what was coming.

'Barfield,' the minister snapped. 'Old Tippet's God-forsaken constituency. Poor devil's run ragged. That shooting of a cleric and the son of a local councillor at the mosque: Tippet could lose his seat. A lot of his constituents are Muslims. You'll know all about the incident, of course.'

'I know of it, Minister, but only what's been in the press. People here think rival factions are using the troubles as a cover for settling old scores.'

'Rival factions?'

'Sunnis and Shias, Minister. Ancient rivalries.'

'Please, Marcus, don't insult my intelligence.' The minister's voice was icy. 'What about the room full of men in Leeds: cut down with a sub-machine gun? And the two fellows murdered in that bed-sit in Bradford? Heard about that? Of course you have. It's that bloody woman you recruited, isn't it?'

Marcus ignored the question. 'You must have read the report in *The Times*, Minister. The police found detonators and more than a ton of ammonium nitrate in the garage of the Leeds house. And we've got the London bombers. Pulled them in last night.'

'Thought they were suicides?'

'We put that about. The bombs were all timer-detonated.'

The minister suddenly realized he was being manipulated. 'Stop trying to sidetrack me, Marcus. What I'm concerned about is old Tippet's constituency. Muslim leader and a councillor's son killed in cold blood? Jesus, Marcus! What's going on?'

'The youth had been taken in for questioning before the troubles, Minister. Trained at an al-Qaeda camp, studied chemistry at Leeds University: we know he was involved in bomb manufacture. And the Barfield cleric was a terrorist recruiter and organizer. Items found at the mosque and in the Bradford bed-sit led us to the London bombers.'

'What about due process?'

'Due process, Minister?'

'Of the law, dammit,' the voice roared down the line. 'You can't send some psychopathic bitch out to kill everyone you have on some bloody list. You arrest the beggars. The emergency powers allow you to hold them indefinitely.'

'I don't understand the point you're trying to make, Minister. The woman I think you're referring to is on surveillance duties. We're pretty sure the killings were the result of some feud within the Muslim community.' Marcus smiled to himself: even Pogmore couldn't have done a better job of winding the silly sod up.

'You must think I fell off the last bus, Marcus,' the minister fumed. 'Anyway, it's things nearer to home that I really want to talk to you about.'

'Nearer to home, Minister?'

'You know she's arranged for some Albanian whores to be taken to a safe house?'

'She? I'm not sure who you're referring to, Minister.'

'For God's sake, Marcus,' the minister exploded. 'That bloody woman you recruited. Some of the girls were under age. I know the people involved have been less than wise, but dammit, Marcus, no one's perfect. Who's to cast the first stone?'

'I've not heard about this, Minister,' Marcus lied. 'Who are these people?'

'Our sort of people,' the minister snapped. 'Decent types. Chairman of the local Conservative Association, a past president of Rotary, a couple of high-ranking police officers, one of them decorated for bravery, businessmen who've contributed generously to the Party. Most of them big fundraisers: hospices, children's homes, cancer, leukaemia; you name it, they've raised funds for it.'

'Pillars of the community,' Markus said, encouragingly.

'You're damn right. Crown Prosecution Service may go for them under the Sex Offences Act. Local police are doing their best to drag their feet, but the woman who phoned and gave the tip off made sure the call was recorded and heard by half the squad at the station. And one of the whores collected all the used condoms for DNA testing. Can you believe it, Marcus? Two buckets of used French letters! That bloody woman put the bitches up to it. Her hallmark's stamped all over it.'

Marcus struggled to hold back the laughter. 'The Albanian ladies seem to have been rather enterprising, Minister. Were the buckets very full?'

'This isn't funny, Marcus.' The voice was icy with rage. 'These are decent people who've devoted their lives to public service. Special people who oil the wheels, organize things, make things happen. Two of them are in my father's old lodge, for heaven's sake. And that bitch might have destroyed them. She's torn the heart out of Barfield: torn its bloody heart out.'

'From what you say, Minister, the girls were very young. Surely we can't condone . . . ?'

'Little Albanian whores. Had more men than you've had hot dinners. It's outrageous for the CPS to talk about sex offences.'

'I'm not sure in what way I can help you,' Marcus said.

The minister let out a resigned sigh. 'I'll have to try and deal with the mess in Barfield, but I want you to get that interfering bitch out of the country. I want her out of the way before the CPS decides to proceed.'

'I think I could arrange that for you, Minister. She wants to transfer back to MI6 and operate abroad, but there's a small obstacle.' Marcus tried to sound helpful. He had to seize this opportunity.

'Obstacle?'

'I raised it with the Foreign Secretary a few weeks ago, but he saw difficulties. Now the situation's worsened, I think he'd view things differently. If you could have a word, minister . . . ?'

*   *   *

'Sorry it took so long, Sam. I thought I had it in the bag this summer, but the Foreign Secretary needed a lot of persuading. Still, you should be back before the Christmas break.'

'It's OK, Marcus. I just want it to be all over.'

Samantha sipped her brandy, relaxing after the very pleasant meal. Glittering with chrome, black glass and mirrors, lit by lots of art deco chandeliers, the restaurant was crammed with city types enjoying expense account lunches. The bustle, the hum of conversation, veiled her in anonymity. She found it comforting.

This was the place she'd brought Ruth Turner for lunch during the summer. Samantha wondered how she was, whether or not she'd entered the religious order. If everything went as planned in Russia, she might pay her a visit.

'You're looking sensational,' Marcus said.

'Sensational?' Samantha laughed huskily. 'Sometimes I'm not quite sure what you're trying to say to me, Marcus.'

'Radiant, then,' Marcus offered. 'I think it could be the tan. And that little Emanuel Ungaro dress is really something. Black suits you.'

She went on laughing, not displeased. 'I'm impressed, Marcus. You knew it was an Ungaro?'

He looked contrite. 'Not really. I cheated. Read the label when I helped you off with your coat.'

Damn, Samantha muttered to herself, then pretended to smooth her hair while she discreetly tucked the offending square of silk under the neckline. Out loud she said, 'Any feedback from surveillance?'

'Feedback?'

'About the deaths in Barfield and here in Leeds and other places north?'

'Not a whisper. Police haven't got anywhere, of course. The constituency MPs keep asking questions in the House and we've put it about that it's rival Muslim factions, but no one seriously believes us.' He suddenly smiled across at her. 'Bet you looked great in a burqa; those fabulous eyes gazing out over the veil.'

'How are your beautiful wife and daughters? Have the girls settled in at Felsham Ladies' College?'

Marcus's smile broadened. He knew he'd had his wrist slapped for flirting. 'They're fine. Doing very well in fact. Parents' day last week: met Sally's new English tutor, we went to school together, chap called Rudd.'

'Rudd?' Samantha began to pay attention.

'Gavin Rudd. Awfully pleasant type. Had a rough time at school: bit bookish, hated games, but he got a first at Oxford. You know him?'

'Fat bald-headed little man?' she said discreetly.

Marcus laughed. 'Heavens, no. Tall, handsome and very charming. Captivated Charlotte, my wife. Made her go all girlish. Headmistress discovered him and persuaded him to join the staff. He's transformed the English department.'

Her gigolo had landed a job at a high-class ladies' college! Samantha tried hard not to smile when she asked, 'How old is the headmistress?'

Marcus shrugged. 'Early forties. Must say, she was much more pleasant at parents' day than when we enrolled the girls. Hardly recognized her. Different woman.'

A pianist began to play Cole Porter tunes: thirties melodies were harmonizing with the thirties decor.

Handing her an envelope, Marcus said, 'Your tickets: British Airways flight to Moscow, tomorrow. Booked you in club class. The Russian military will take over after Moscow and fly you out to the prison. Names and photographs of the people who'll meet you are in the envelope.'

'Club class! You're making free with the extra funding.'

'The chief's grateful, Sam.' Marcus caught a waiter's eye and asked for the bill.

'Did Vrakimi and Karlensa have any terrorist connections?'

'Nothing significant. Karlensa had supplied some Artane to a fundamentalist group in Bradford, that's all.'

'Artane?'

'Benzhexol. Anti-psychotic drug. Supposed to give a feeling of invincibility. Bombers often take it before they go on a mission.'

'How are Maria Vrakimi and the girls?'

Marcus looked down at his plate, began to move the remains of his desert around with a fork. 'They're in transit camp six, near Dover, waiting for the deportation orders to be signed.'

Samantha frowned, put her elbows on the table and leant towards him. 'They were in a safe house in Sunderland, waiting to give evidence,' she snapped.

He tried to meet the green blaze of her eyes. 'The CPS aren't proceeding. They don't see any real chance of those fellows in Barfield being convicted.'

'They've got the girls as witnesses; they've got semen samples. I'd have thought it was an open and shut case.'

Marcus sighed. 'The girls can hardly speak English. Lawyers at the CPS have interviewed them and they don't think they'll make reliable witnesses.'

'What about the semen?'

'The accused all had cute lawyers. They refused to be tested for a match.'

'Could they refuse?'

'Not sure. Either way, they managed to delay things until the samples went missing between the police station and the laboratory.'

'Bet the minister had to work hard on that one,' Samantha said bitterly.

Unable to meet her gaze, Marcus went on making patterns in the chocolate sauce with his fork.

'Is it worth it, Marcus?' she asked huskily.

'I don't know what you mean.'

'What are we trying to defend? The freedom to cheat and fornicate? Fixers, wheeler-dealers; the right of the great and good to put themselves beyond the law? Jesus, Marcus, why should I risk life and sanity for those corrupt bastards? All the terrorists I've dispatched these past four months, at least they're fighting for a cause, not having sex with little girls in pigtails and party frocks.'

'Steady on, Sam.' A blushing Marcus glanced around the neighbouring tables, horrified she might have been overheard.

'You're not being reasonable. Without the freedom to indulge in vice there can be no virtue. And all societies have hierarchies: people who think they're special, networkers who get involved and take control.'

'Turds floating to the top in the cesspool,' Samantha muttered. 'And we're the shit-shovellers, clearing up the mess the arrogant bastards leave behind after they've taken what they want.'

Marcus laughed. 'You've a penchant for the scatological metaphor, Sam. Don't be bitter. They oil the wheels, and lusting after little girls isn't confined to the great and the good.'

He studied her face. This woman would walk up to the cannon's mouth. She was the best operative he'd ever had. But the years of killing were extracting a toll. She was on the edge. He could see it in those chillingly beautiful eyes and the hard set of her mouth.

From across the room, above the murmur of conversation, came the tinkling refrain of 'Every Time We Say Goodbye'. The pianist was weaving a spell. Marcus listened to a few bars, then said softly, 'Anyway, the ruction you caused gave me the leverage I needed to arrange the Russian trip for you.'

'I don't follow.'

'They want you out of the country, Sam.'

'I've really got up their noses, haven't I? I'll bet they're party fund-raisers, people who went to the right schools then joined the right clubs. Maybe one or two are on the new-year's honours list. I thought we were all part of a democratic meritocracy, Marcus. All equal under the law?'

Marcus began making patterns in the chocolate sauce again. 'It's the system, Sam. It's the way things work.'

Samantha began to laugh.

He glanced up and relief was evident in his voice as he said, 'Thanks for taking it so well, Sam. I thought you'd be outraged.'

Reaching beneath the table, she lifted a crimson Gucci bag and pressed its big gilt clasp. She took out a package and placed it in front of him. 'Give that to the head of the Crown Prosecution Service and suggest he invites the minister over for a viewing.'

Marcus looked from package to Samantha and raised his eyebrows.

'It's a video. Vrakimi monitored all the rooms from an office in the attic. Maybe he had blackmail in mind. I took two sacks of the things. Tell them to scroll through to the 6th, 13th and 20th of May. If the women and girls aren't back in the safe house and the CPS back on the job before Christmas, the media get the rest of the tapes. And if they start talking sequestration, remind them Maria is Vrakimi's widow.'

Laughing softly, she tossed her napkin on to the table, rose to her feet, and made her way through the chattering diners to the cloakroom near the entrance. Marcus followed.

'You expected it, didn't you, Sam?' He helped her on with her scarlet winter coat. Its silk lining felt cool against her bare arms as he settled it around her shoulders.

She turned and looked at him. 'I'd have been amazed if they hadn't closed ranks and tried to bury this one.'

A waiter dragged the heavy chrome and glass door open. Samantha shivered, suddenly chilled by the freezing gloom of the damp December afternoon.

CHAPTER EIGHTEEN

The co-pilot slid the door aside, then jumped down on to the snow, and Samantha was enveloped in a cold that was deadly in its intensity. Through the open door, the howl of gas turbines was deafening, almost drowning the sound of idling rotors beating against the freezing air.

She wrapped her furs around her, walked to

the edge of the metal deck and looked out. The co-pilot was reaching up. Leaning forward, she allowed herself to fall, felt his hands around her waist as he caught her and lowered her on to the snow.

In the glare of the landing lights, beyond the circle of churning air, stood the general in a khaki greatcoat with crimson piping. The crimson band and gold laurel leaves on the upswept peak of his cap, his crimson and gold epaulettes, added splashes of vivid colour. Dressed that way, his bulk and stature made him an impressive figure.

Samantha stooped under the down draught from swirling rotors and crunched across fresh snow towards him. Coming close, she studied the big Slavonic features: bushy black eyebrows over glittering eyes, big broad nose, flat cheeks, hard mouth. She was looking at a well fed, clean-shaven version of the battle-weary man she remembered from Chechnya.

'It is wonderful to see you again,' he said gruffly.

'And you, General.'

Turning abruptly, he led her down a narrow footway, plunging into the darkness beyond the glare of the landing lights. They were moving between low buildings built from rough concrete blocks, snow beneath their feet, a ribbon of sky bright with stars above their heads.

The footway widened. Light, escaping

through a parting in double doors, gleamed across the snow. The general climbed rough wooden steps and pushed through the opening. In the sudden spill of light, Samantha saw uniformed guards standing to attention on either side of the doorway. She followed the general into a dingy latrine block.

Three naked bulbs were hanging down from the rafters, their feeble light emphasizing the primitive nature of the place. Wash basins, mounted back to back, ran down the centre of the block. On the left, a dozen water closets, without lids or seats, were ranged along a white-tiled wall. The wall on the right was coated with tar up to chest height to form a continuous urinal. A couple of cast iron radiators were doing no more than protect the plumbing from freezing. They made the stench worse.

When the general moved his vast bulk aside, Samantha could see to the far end of the block. They'd chained the man, arms outstretched across the tiling, to rusty iron pipes that rose up the wall.

'Do you wish me to stay?' The general's words came on misty clouds in the freezing air.

Samantha shook her head and began to walk over slimy concrete towards the chained figure. She heard the doors close behind her, then stopped within two paces of the bearded man in baggy white trousers and a collarless shirt. His legs were shackled together, just above the boot tops, by a metal bar, and fearful eyes were watching her through a fall of lank black hair.

'You are Ahmed Nasari, an American national?' Her voice echoed down the long building.

'I do not understand. I have no English,' he said in Arabic.

Samantha studied him closely. He looked much older than she remembered. Unkempt hair and a heavy growth of beard, dim light and the ammonia-like stench stinging her eyes, made recognition difficult. Behind her, a tap was dripping into a half-filled basin. Faintly, beyond the buildings, she could hear the beat of rotor blades, the whine of helicopter turbines; they wouldn't dare shut them down in the arctic cold.

Stepping forward, she tugged the thick shirt and a couple of vests out of his pants. The beginning of the scar was there, just above his hip. She had to be sure. She grabbed the waistband of his pants, tore them open and pulled them down around his thighs. A red weal, crossed by faint stitch marks, snaked across his stomach and plunged into the hair around his groin. She was looking at field surgery, carried out by an al-Qaeda amateur in a cave in Afghanistan. It was Nasari. She had no doubt of it now.

Samantha stepped back. 'You know who I am?' she asked.

He grinned his contempt at her. 'I knew you were coming when they chained me here. I've been waiting for you.' He'd dropped the pretence. His American accent was pronounced.

They stared at one another in silence across the freezing space.

Eventually he said, 'I almost killed you. Once when you crossed the border into Pakistan; once when you were going up to that apartment you had in Paris. You were laden with shopping, I had you in the sights, and then a lorry passed. When it had gone you'd vanished into the building. After that I was always running from the police and the security services.'

Nasari, the last man, standing before her in the stinking communal latrines of a Siberian prison. She thought of her sister and her sister's child, of the brother-in-law whose face she scarcely remembered. Reaching inside her furs, she drew out the gun and stepped back half-a-dozen paces, well clear of any spurting blood.

Tears were coursing down her cheeks and her body was shaking, convulsed by a bewildering mixture of emotions: rage, guilt, sadness, loss, relief at the prospect of release from fear. Feet apart, she gripped the gun in both hands, raised it and aimed.

Nasari threw back his head and screamed, 'There is no god but Allah and Muhammad is

His . . .'

The first bullet hit him in the shoulder; the second tore a hole in his cheek. When his body sagged forward on the chains she emptied the magazine into the bowed head.

Samantha stepped back, gripped the rim of a washbasin, and stared at blood-streaked tiles, the mess of blood and brains and splintered bone.

'It is accomplished,' a gruff voice murmured softly.

She turned. The general was standing close behind her. He ignored her tears and the convulsive shaking of her body; offered her no word or hand in comfort. He was a soldier. He understood.

Dragging in the stinking air, fighting for self-control, she asked, 'Will you have him buried?'

The general smiled, shook his head, and pointed towards the floor with a gloved finger. 'Permafrost,' he grunted, then turned towards the doors and barked an order.

Uniformed guards clattered in, boots scraping on the concrete. The general nodded towards the body and said, 'Bring him.'

He helped her down the steps, offered his arm as they walked back along the narrow footway. The guards followed, dragging Nasari's body, feet first, through the snow.

A figure, silhouetted against the landing lights, was stumbling towards them. 'Hurry,

General. The weather: if we stay any longer we'll never leave.'

The guards heaved the now unshackled body on to the metal decking while the pilot reached down, gripped Samantha's hands, and lifted her on board. He peered towards the shadowy outlines of the buildings, becoming more agitated. She couldn't hear him over the whine of the engines, but she watched his mouth shaping the words, 'Where the devil is he?'

'The general is joining us?' Samantha asked, yelling above the din.

'Accompanying you back to Moscow. He flew out, two days ago, to meet you here.'

The general's huge bulk appeared out of the shadows. He stooped, held his cap, and the down draught tugged at his coat as he ran beneath the rotors. The two guards followed, carrying an ammunition case.

Pilot and co-pilot each grabbed an arm and heaved the general aboard, then they took the metal case from the guards, slid the door shut and scrambled through to the controls.

The whine of the turbines rose in pitch, the beat of the rotors became more frantic. Samantha felt the machine lurch upwards and the general held her arm while she found her seat.

He sat facing her and glanced at his watch. 'Five minutes and we'll throw Nasari out. The wolves will celebrate Christmas early.

Meanwhile . . .' he lifted the lid of the ammunition case, '. . . we will have a little celebration of our own.' He beamed at Samantha, then peered down into the case.

They'd gained height and the engines were no longer straining. With the door closed, the rudimentary sound-proofing specially installed in the cavernous transport ship made it possible to hold a conversation without shouting.

'French champagne, Russian brandy, chicken, caviar, a little salad and . . .' he searched amongst the contents '. . . butter and fresh bread.'

'Fresh bread?'

'It was baked here this morning. Supervised by the governor himself. Perfectly wholesome; the prisoners on the kitchen rota would not dare contaminate it with the governor watching.'

The general suddenly became serious. Reaching over and taking her hand, he said, 'It's good to see you again, Samantha. I don't forget who brought me success in Chechnya, who handed me my promotion.'

'You earned the promotion, General.'

He shrugged. 'I'm not the only one who has cause to be grateful. Interior Minister Grazyev would not be so highly regarded were it not for your efforts against the terror.' He gestured towards the case.

'Brandy,' Samantha said.

He found a couple of glasses, wrapped in a napkin, and uncorked the bottle. Then he glanced up at her and said, 'You lead a life that is full of danger and uncertainty. Tonight you have removed a threat, but there will be others in the future. If you ever need a refuge, Grazyev would arrange for you to have a flat in Moscow, secure you a pension.' He laughed. 'It would be small by western standards, but it would be something. And you could use my dacha, take tea with my wife, talk English with my son and daughter.'

'I'm touched, General. You're more than kind.' Samantha unfastened the voluminous fur coat, reached into an inner pocket and found the document and package Marcus had given her. She handed the papers over. 'The transfer document for Nasari.'

'I forgot!' He placed the bottle and glasses back in the case, rose and dragged Nasari's body to the edge of the deck. When he eased open the door they were buffeted by noise and freezing air. He rolled the body out into the darkness and crashed the door shut.

After he'd resumed his seat, Samantha said, 'Marcus asked me to give you this.' She handed him the small package.

He beamed. 'Perfume,' he said. 'For Irina, my wife. She adores such things. Marcus sends it to me from time to time.' He retrieved the bottle and glasses. 'Shall we pass the time eating and drinking and making toasts?'

He handed her a napkin and filled her glass. 'A toast to your Queen?' He studied her expression. 'No? To her government, perhaps?'

Samantha rolled her eyes upwards.

The general roared with laughter. 'It is the same in Russia: the same the world over. You choose.'

'We should toast people of real importance,' Samantha said. She raised her glass. 'To your beautiful wife and children.'

He beamed, slapped a huge knee. 'But of course. To Irina and Alexander and Sophia.'

They downed the brandy in a single swallow. Samantha closed her eyes, felt the reviving glow burning through her.

Leaning forward, the general refilled her glass. 'Choose another,' he insisted.

Samantha pondered for a few moments, listening to the muffled howl of the turbines. Then she raised her glass and said, 'Justice for the meek.'

The huge Halo cargo ship sped southwards over starlit ice fields. Beneath them, wolves were tearing at the body of Ahmed Nasari.

*   *   *

Samantha pointed the Ferrari up the rise to the south of Sheffield and left the heavy Christmas traffic behind. Grimy sandstone villas gave way to modern brick houses. She passed a school, a water tower, and then she was driving between bleak fields that bordered the moors.

She saw the gatehouse up ahead, turned between stone pillars and drove down the side of a high enclosing wall that was massively buttressed. After parking the car outside a gothic chapel as big as a parish church, she gathered up her packages and walked around the building until she found the convent entrance. A sign beneath the porch said, "Ring and Enter". She rang and entered.

The tiny vestibule was bare save for a curtained grille in the wall facing the entrance door. After a few minutes she heard movement behind the grille and a refined female voice said, 'May I help you?'

'I'd like to see Miss Turner; Ruth Turner.'

'Visiting is discouraged during Advent. Perhaps after Christmas?'

Samantha moved closer to the grille and tried to discern a face through the curtain. 'I've traveled from Siberia. After Christmas I may no longer be in England. Could you relax the rules?'

'From Siberia?' The nun's voice registered no surprise. 'I suppose the Reverend Mother might make an exception. Who am I to say is calling?'

'Quest; Samantha Quest.'

'Would you go through the door on your left, up the stairs and through the first door you come to. It's the small parlour.' She chuckled. 'Siberia! I suppose it's awfully cold there?'

'Almost as cold as it is in here,' Samantha said wryly, and heard the nun laughing as she moved away from the grille.

Cream walls, brown woodwork, bare boards. Samantha removed her black satin Blahnik shoes and carried them, concerned that the stiletto heels might scar the oak stairs. Entering the parlour, she was confronted by another metal grille, this one shuttered on the far side and reaching almost to the low ceiling. Beneath it was a deep drawer, put there so gifts of food could be passed through to the enclosure.

A Windsor chair faced the grille. Placing her packages and shoes beside it, she sat down, crossed her legs, and waited.

Minutes passed, then the shutters clattered open, and Ruth Turner was staring out at her. 'It really is you!'

Samantha rose, came closer to the grille while the novice settled herself on the polished boards: there was no furniture of any kind on the convent side. The girl was dressed in a habit of coarse brown cloth, her head concealed beneath a tightly fitting white cotton hood that left only her face exposed: she would not wear the black outer mantle until she was professed.

'I came to say hello and to see how you are.'

Ruth smiled up at her. 'I'm fine. I entered Carmel in September.'

'You really are OK?'

'I've never been so happy. Honestly!'

'I hope it lasts,' Samantha said, without irony.

'I'll have my dark night of the soul, I suppose, but I'm just living for the day.'

Dark night of the soul: I could write the book, Samantha mused to herself.

'How are your parents?'

'They really have parted now,' Ruth sighed. 'Daddy found someone else and mummy's been very quiet and sad about it. She didn't seem all that bothered when daddy first left, but she suddenly became very depressed in the summer. I thought it was because I was entering Carmel, but she insisted it wasn't. She comes to see me most weeks. She's coming on Christmas Day with daddy; visiting starts again then.'

Samantha gazed through the bars at the girl sitting on the floor. Big bright eyes, rosy cheeks, tiny nose and the rather full smiling mouth that was saying how pleased she was with her situation.

Becoming uncomfortable under the silent scrutiny, Ruth stopped smiling and said, 'That's a splendid coat. Huge; all that silver fur massed around the shoulders, and it almost trails along the floor.' She was only making conversation.

'Siberian wolf,' Samantha said absently. 'The pelts were sewn in Paris. It was a gift from the Russian people.'

Ruth's eyebrows lifted. Could there be any wolves left in Siberia after the making of such a coat, she wondered.

Samantha remembered the girl's indifference to clothes and guessed she was trying to conceal her distaste at the outrageous display of vanity.

'If you like it, I'll give it to you.'

Ruth laughed. 'What would I do with a fur coat?'

'You could sleep in it.'

The girl nodded enthusiastically. 'It would certainly keep out the cold.'

Samantha smiled. 'Do you still sleep on sacks stuffed with straw.'

'How do you know about that?'

'I get around.'

'Not any more,' Ruth said. 'It's been ordinary beds for years now, but it can be cold.'

They gazed at one another through the bars for a while then, once more embarrassed by the silence, Ruth asked, 'The band of stones around the neckline of your dress and around the cuffs; are they really diamonds?'

Samantha shook her head. 'Black velvet Versace dress, but the stones are paste.'

'Will you spend Christmas with your family?'

'I don't have a family,' Samantha said. 'I used to spend holidays with my sister, her husband and my niece, but they're all dead.'

'I'm sorry.' Ruth frowned up at her.

'Don't be. It's an issue I resolved yesterday. I'm moving on now.'

'What's the real reason you've come to see me?'

Samantha studied the rosy-cheeked face. The girl had the innocence, the acute perception, of a child, and she couldn't think of an answer. 'To bring you these,' Samantha said, gesturing towards the packages.

The girl shuffled towards the grille and pushed out the drawer.

Samantha laid the packages inside. 'Beluga caviar, Russian brandy and Belgian chocolate.'

Ruth pulled the drawer into the enclosure. 'You're very kind. Thank you. What's caviar like?'

Samantha wrinkled her nose. 'Acquired taste. A little on toast sometimes works as a hangover cure.'

'We don't have hangovers.'

'You will if you drink the brandy. The Russian army uses it for unfreezing tank tracks.'

'Really!'

Samantha laughed huskily. 'I'm kidding. I prefer it to the French. It's sweeter, mellower.'

Ruth began to lift out the packages. 'You'll be cooking Christmas dinner?' she asked, making conversation again.

'I don't cook, I don't dust and I don't clean. I just bathe, wear fine clothes and go about my business. Your Reverend Mother wouldn't care for me at all.'

'She'd care for *anybody*,' Ruth said brightly, unaware of the put-down.

Samantha laughed.

'And your business is buying furniture for hotels?' Ruth said, then smiled.

Samantha just smiled back.

'Why did you come?' the girl asked again. 'What do you really want?'

Samantha stepped close to the grille. Slender fingers with scarlet nails grasped the black metal. She put her face with its discreetly shadowed eyes and scarlet lips close to the bars so she could have an unobstructed view of the girl in the habit of brown wool. She'd wanted to see her, make sure she was OK; she'd wanted to give her the festive things she'd acquired on her travels; but she knew these weren't the real reasons she'd been drawn to the place, and she was too exhausted to analyse her feelings. And how did you express such things in a few words?

She gazed down at the girl for a dozen heartbeats, then said softly, 'Salvation.'

Ruth's eyes widened. 'If you want it you already have it.' Samantha smiled. 'Is it as simple as that?'

'I believe so.'

Samantha continued to look down at her. There would probably be an older nun, sitting with her back to the wall, out of sight of the grille. The Mother Superior wouldn't allow a novice to see a strange visitor alone. And, later, Ruth might be given a gentle talk on the doctrine of redemption.

'Then I'll have to ask for a peaceful death.'

'I'll pray for you,' Ruth said. She rose to her feet. 'Will you come and see me again?'

'Would you like that?' Samantha asked.

'Of course. I'd see some more French haute couture.' She laughed happily.

*   *   *

Snow was falling through the fading light when Samantha stepped out of the convent and climbed into the car. It might linger up here on the moors, but it would turn to slush on the city streets.

Driving through Sheffield, stopping and starting beneath flashing stars and reindeers, Merry Christmases and Santas, she read the evening news hoardings: "Underage Immigrant Girls Used for Sex; Ten Charged".

Her mood lifted a little. She toyed fleetingly with finding Maria, joining her and the other women for the Christmas break. She decided against it. The gentlemen of the press would make sure they were well provided for in return for a story.

She'd get a frozen dinner before the stores closed and find the instruction book for that microwave thing. Chill out with a few drinks, clean and oil her gun, prepare for the coming year.

We hope you have enjoyed this Large Print book. Other Chivers Press or Thorndike Press Large Print books are available at your library or directly from the publishers.

For more information about current and forthcoming titles, please call or write, without obligation, to:

Chivers Large Print
published by BBC Audiobooks Ltd
St James House, The Square
Lower Bristol Road
Bath BA2 3BH
UK
email: bbcaudiobooks@bbc.co.uk
www.bbcaudiobooks.co.uk

OR

Thorndike Press
295 Kennedy Memorial Drive
Waterville
Maine 04901
USA
www.gale.com/thorndike
www.gale.com/wheeler

All our Large Print titles are designed for easy reading, and all our books are made to last.